THE CIGAR ROLLER

PABLO MEDINA

THE CIGAR ROLLER

Grove Press
New York

Published simultaneously in Canada
Printed in the United States of America

FIRST EDITION

Library of Congress Cataloging-in-Publication Data

Medina, Pablo, 1948–
The cigar roller : a novel / by Pablo Medina.

p. cm.

ISBN 0-8021-1792-9

1. Cerebrovascular disease—Patients—Fiction.   2. Hospital patients—Fiction.
3. Cuban Americans—Fiction.   4. Cigar industry—Fiction.   5. Havana
(Cuba)—Fiction.   6. Paralytics—Fiction.   8. Florida—Fiction.   I. Title.
PS3563.E24C54 2005
813'.54—dc22   2004054141

Grove Press
an imprint of Grove/Atlantic, Inc.
841 Broadway
New York, NY 10003

05 06 07 08 09   10 9 8 7 6 5 4 3 2 1

In Memory of Carlos Medina Unanue

Courage is not enough to learn the art of forgetting.
—*Jorge Luis Borges*

The imperfect is our paradise.
—*Wallace Stevens*

Amadeo Terra is staring out the window to the sea on which the sun is dancing. He looks out and he looks in and he remembers the day he landed on these shores with his wife and three children and his youngest tugging at his sleeve, asking the impertinent questions young boys ask and their fathers cannot answer without revealing the depth of their ignorance. Amadeo Terra remembers how he pushed the boy away, too forcefully it seems now, too much like a man trying to prove himself—to a child no less—and how the boy ran to cling to his mother's dress. Amadeo Terra can do nothing but remember.

Two white canvas straps, one around his chest, the other around his lap, keep him in his chair. His body has not moved for four years and seven months. He remembers walking on a sunny street, cigar smoke curling upward from his mouth. He remembers his brain shutting down, his cheek on the sidewalk, his left arm twisted behind him. He remembers thinking that just when he had it all—money, a comfortable house, a new car—somebody dropped an anvil on him. Life arriving. Life escaping. Ridiculous. The sun is dappling the chops on the bay and he is finding patterns to the glinting light where none exist. At first it is like a musical beat—ta-ta, ta ta-ta—then it is a street full of neon signs blinking on and off and then it becomes a summer night in the country after the fireflies hatch. Cocuyos—that's the Cuban name—thousands of them over the field behind the house. Occasionally a motorboat speeds by, cutting the water and leaving a wake of foam behind. Sometimes a boat will be pulling a skier. The skier crosses the wake, skipping over it then turning and crossing the wake again and again until boat and skier disappear behind the frame of the window. Much of the time there are birds, large slow soaring ones with scissor tails and small streaking ones that fly in a straight line. If he strains he can see a long bridge in the distance and beyond it sailboats floating off gracefully into the open sea. Storms appear often enough, usually in the afternoon, and he likes to watch as the sky darkens and the lightning flashes out at the edges of the sea. Once a waterspout formed over the bay, crossed the causeway on the right and plowed through a stand of pines on the mainland. Mostly, however, it is the sun shining on the water, and he likes that best of all. Time ago, he awoke early enough to see the large cargo ships lumbering out of the harbor at high tide. Time before that he was on a boat himself sailing into the harbor, sails at full mast, the prow sending spray over him and his children, Julia complaining, the sailors cursing. It was the greatest morning of his life, nothing but wide sky and stars and the future ahead.

At five o'clock Nurse brings to the rolling table by his chair a tray with several jars of baby food, some warm, some cool. She is a master of efficiency, everything placed on the tray in its proper order—the bib, the jars, the spoon, the towel, the plastic juice bottle, like a child's, in the shape of a bear. She opens the first jar, split pea with ham, swirls it with a teaspoon a few times, then tests it for warmth by tapping some on the back of her hand. Amadeo Terra follows her motions with his eyes as he has done every day since he's been here. He wants to speak, he wants her to see him trying to speak, but she does not like him drooling while he eats and so he doesn't try. Instead he allows her to slip the spoon into his mouth. There, that's good, she says wiping the excess off his lips with one sweep of the teaspoon. Sometimes, when his mind doesn't play tricks on him, he imagines what it was like to eat real food— steak, rare, with yuca fried in lard and half a loaf of bread, or his favorite, enchilado de jaibas with a bowl of rice and plantains on the side, washed down with beer. He had gotten fat, a full three hundred pounds in his prime. A man eats. There were days when he consumed six servings of paella for lunch and two steaks for dinner, and there were days when he was working so hard he ate like a nun, a ham sandwich, a bowl of soup. He ruled his appetites, not the other way around. Now he is being fed baby food. How he longs for a large piece of bovine flesh, stringy with sinew and marbled with fat, how he dreams every day of thick pork chops, oozing with grease. He cannot bite, he cannot chew, he cannot grab the ribs with his hands. When he first arrived at the home they pulled all his teeth. He remembers how easily they slipped out of his gums, one by one, with barely a jiggle of the dentist's clamp, then the sound of them clanging in the metal basin. The teeth were not worth fixing, they said, and feeding him would be easier that way. Mush, that is, baby food, a little apple juice, on occasion a cracker he can suck on. Meat, he can only dream of meat.

Nurse thrusts another spoonful in his mouth. He barely tastes the split pea and swallows quickly. She follows with something sweet—a flavor he cannot recall. He blinks once, yes, and swirls the paste around and won't swallow again until he can recognize it, something from his childhood, when taste was an adjunct of eating. The substance is familiar to him on his lips, on the tip of his tongue, on the tissues of the inside of his mouth, its aroma filling his nostrils, a substance like a yellow light in his brain. His mouth is clamped in concentration and just as he is about to name the taste, just as he is about to grasp the truth, Nurse tries to force the split pea through his lips. He blinks twice, no, and keeps his jaw shut; he is almost there. She jabs his gums several times with the spoon all the while coaxing him to open up, open up now, I don't have all day, open up. You shouldn't be this selfish, the others need me. Open up. He avoids her eyes and voice, gentle and cheery, riding a crest of impatience, and concentrates on the taste that has filled his mouth, spread up his nostrils, and taken over his whole being. He can smell the past, smell his childhood, pungent and silky, see the sun through the branches of the tree he hid behind until his father tired of looking for him and headed home with anger swelling his forehead. He can smell the grove where he ate fruit that night and got so full he couldn't breathe. He can smell the sap oozing out of the tree trunks.

Nurse is pressing with her thumb and middle finger on his mandible. She has done this before. Mostly she succeeded but sometimes, on days when he felt particularly strong, he could keep his jaw clamped and she would, after a time, leave to feed the others, waiting like baby birds for her and her jars. But she wouldn't leave quietly. Nurse always had to have the last word. As she capped the jars and wiped the rolling table, she would say in a calm, condescending tone that he was ungrateful, that he was taking too much of her time, that next time she would send the orderly to feed him. Amadeo Terra is willing to resist forever, have her pack her jars, her bib and her spoon and take them to her next case, willing to starve himself (as if that process hadn't already begun) in order to find in his memory the source of that taste. And just as Nurse is wiping his face one last time in her mock anger (she doesn't really care whether Amadeo eats or not, sleeps or not, lives or not) mango appears. He swallows, closes his eyes. Mango. Yellow, pulpy, stringy, sticky yellow. Mango! He wants it, tubs of it, he wants all mango, mango day and mango night, mango moon and mango sun and mango sea and mango mountain and mango swamp. Nurse is mango. Home is mango. Amadeo Terra is mango. He opens his mouth wide, he wants mango. The fat around his throat is quivering for more. Mango, he yells with his eyes; mango, he begs, blinking yes.

Nurse notices, thinks she has won and Amadeo is repentant. She smiles triumphantly. She rolls the table back into place, sits on the chair by the bed. Amadeo still has his mouth open but now his whole being strains with the effort. If he could chirp, he would. He follows her actions with his eyes, watches as she places the tray with the jars on the table. The bib, don't forget the bib. She starts with the split pea, spooning it in quickly and efficiently, as if she were feeding a coal furnace rather than a human being. Amadeo obliges, swallowing, anticipating. He is ready to do anything, eat lead if he has to, in order to get more of the sweet taste of mango. She collects the last of the split pea, sweeping inside the jar with the spoon, and jabs it deep in his mouth. She caps the empty jar and searches blindly for another, picks one that bears no resemblance to yellow, and begins to open it. Amadeo tries to warn her with his eyes, not mango, not mango, but she realizes it is still sealed, puts it back, and finds the mango finally. Amadeo has never felt such desire, not even as a young man when the whole world was desire. By the time she opens the jar, he is close to tears. The taste is different now, more like sky, not sea, more skin, light inside a pocket, breast in water. If he closes his eyes it is a deep blue; when he opens them he tastes canary tongue, rain shoulder, tree semen.

As soon as she's done, Nurse leaves the room. No good-bye. Without Nurse there is window, there is sea and sun, there is Amadeo sitting on the chair, but there is no mango. Still, he is happy he no longer has to listen to her baby talk, her empty nurse's voice, the rise and fall of her condescension. He doesn't have to see her big breasts tight against her uniform or hear the rustle of her thighs walking in or smell her perfume and her skin, the white hugeness of it, and her mouth red and incessant and her wormy lips. For a long time he wanted her, spent nights awake imagining what she looked like under all that white cloth, what she would do if he asked—take off her girdle, straddle his face. That was long ago when there was hope. Now he wants to see her as little as possible.

It is mango he wants, the yellow of it on his face and its childhood taste in his mouth again. He remembers a woman once who tasted like mango. It dripped out of her like sun syrup. He remembers the juice on her belly, he remembers sex, the pump and flex, the sea inside him emptying. He remembers running; he remembers Julia his wife in the kitchen, the void in his heart, the mango woman, the bile pushing up his throat; he remembers the china chest crashing to the floor; he remembers Julia holding their son in her arms like a broken doll, the darkness of the night, the next day, the years ahead. All he can do is remember and remember and remember until his eyes close, there before the window, facing the sea on which the sun is dancing, and the taste of everything in his mouth.

It was a Sunday. Amadeo remembers. It was a Sunday and things were quiet and dismal: the port with its ragged wooden buildings, the unpaved streets, the stevedores who milled about like tired fish, still smelling of the night before. The sun had burned away the morning haze and witch-water was already rising from the sandy road that lined the harbor. On the other side of the street a cluster of tobacco warehouses leaned against each other, and at the corner formed by a road that stretched inland away from the port, a lone coconut palm grew, its base painted white. Amadeo fought his disappointment and walked off the pier bearing on his shoulders a steamer trunk that held all of the family's possessions: clothing mostly, a candelabrum, the few pieces of jewelry Julia insisted on bringing with her, a fry pan, five forks, six table spoons, and a book that had belonged to Julia's grandmother entitled *Obras de piedad*. Amadeo was close to six feet tall, broad-shouldered and heavy-armed, and, despite the weight of the trunk, he walked with long certain strides that gave the impression that he knew where he was going.

Julia followed behind him. She was wearing a plain cream-colored muslin dress with a brown silk vest and a beige bonnet—to keep her hair in place during the crossing, she said—that seemed out of place on her head. Was that the way she was dressed? Amadeo is thinking. Maybe it was the gray dress she wore to church. Or one she had bought for the trip. It had gotten soiled on board the ship, and it worried her that she would have to arrive in the United States looking like a Turkish peddler, but that concern was soon to be supplanted by much more immediate ones. She was carrying a gunny sack containing the remains of two slabs of tasajo, a small tin of crackers, a bunch of bananas, and a butcher knife wrapped in cloth. Her full name was Julia González Herrera and she walked with the posture of a woman used to better things and a better life. She had never been on a boat before and the overnight crossing had left her exhausted, with her nerves frayed from the seasickness, the vomiting, the not knowing where they were in the middle of the bobbing darkness, the dampness, the cold waves spraying over the prow, and the awful feeling that she was leaving behind everything she knew and was entering the voracious mouth of fate. It was the worst night of her life, she kept reminding Amadeo through the years, and refused to set foot on a boat again. If her husband wanted to travel, so be it, but he would do it alone. True islander that she was, she mistrusted the sea and sensed that nothing good came from it. The trip from Havana to Tampa had only confirmed her mistrust, given it a firm basis in experience, so that she did not return to the island until many years later, when she thought she was dying.

The boys hovered around her, except Albertico, the youngest, who rushed up to his father and tried to grab his pant leg and was ignored for his effort. Julia yelled out her husband's name, Amadeo!, in alarm but then composed herself and said nothing else. It was the wrong time for anything but the essential questions. Those questions were foremost on Amadeo's mind as well and so she did not need to ask them. Amadeo walked to the end of the pier, crossed the road and, once on the wooden sidewalk, set the trunk down and wiped his forehead with the back of his hand. He looked back and saw his wife already wilting in the heat. She crossed the street with Albertico holding on to her skirt and the other two close behind her, and for a brief moment it occurred to Amadeo that all of this was a mistake, that they should have stayed on the island and braved the authorities, but it was not a thought that held. What's done is done. A lo hecho pecho.

When Julia reached him, he told her to wait there, and he entered a bodega where a group of stevedores were gathered having their morning brandy. Julia had the two oldest boys move the trunk under the tree at the corner. She sat on it, pulled the knife from the burlap sack and cut up the rest of the tasajo, placing the pieces on the lard crackers and handing them to the children. Only Rubén, the oldest, refused to eat the dry meat, claiming his stomach hurt, and Julia offered him a banana. The other boys, too young to name their fears, had been trained by their father not to linger over their food, and so they ate their share without speaking. Finally, when the children were fed, Julia took out her rosary from her dress pocket and began to say it, more out of habit than religious conviction. It was one of the many practices she had acquired when she had almost miscarried her firstborn and had been ordered to stay in bed for the duration of the pregnancy. She had also learned embroidery and had read many books, but the only habit she retained, being the most portable, was the rosary. She had heard a priest say that she didn't need beads, if she could only keep the count of prayers in her head, and that seven rosaries in seven days for seven weeks would buy her a plenary indulgence in perpetuity, but when the priest warned that if she miscounted she would have to start over, she decided she would do it rosary in hand.

The rosary she used had also belonged to her grand-mother, a saintly but morose woman who had died of tuberculosis when Julia was eleven and had imprinted in the girl a number of indelible phobias, among them the fear of the open ocean, that would dominate her actions for the remainder of her life. Amadeo mocked her, saying that with so much praying she wouldn't have time to commit any sins, but she persisted, carrying the rosary everywhere she went—the market, the Chinese laundry, the butcher shop—saying the prayers under her breath, and accomplished the monumental feat of devotion six months before leaving the island.

Julia finished two rosaries and was considering starting a third when Amadeo came out of the bodega accompanied by a short, energetic man with a spring to his step and a Castilian lisp to his voice. The man had a gold front tooth which glinted in the sun and when Amadeo introduced him to Julia, he bent over and kissed her hand like a gentleman, a perfect gentleman as the phrase goes, which she could tell from the white linen suit with silk-lined lapels, the diamond pinky ring, and the precious way he held out his hand, that he was not. He took her hand with three fingers, then bent over at the waist in a deep bow, taking off his bowler with his free hand and bringing it to his chest in a sweeping arc. He said his name was Sergio Reinaldo Ramos but most people called him Chano. As he talked she could smell the alcohol on his breath and, with her empty stomach and the fatigue from the long sea voyage, she felt nauseated and faint and had to cover her nose with her handkerchief to keep from gagging. The action could not have been lost on the dandy.

Chano here, Amadeo said, is recommending me for a job at the Príncipe de Gales factory. Chano squared his shoulders and smiled down at her. As a roller? asked Julia. She may have loved Amadeo unconditionally but she was not above doubting him. She had told him in Havana, when he first brought up the idea after being threatened by the Spanish soldiers, that the trip to el Norte was going to be a travail. That seemed absolutely clear to her now, sitting on the trunk in public, her children without a roof over their heads, and her husband brimming with drink. As a leaf stripper, Amadeo said. Chano added that as soon as there was an opening, he could move up. He had to wait his turn like everyone else. Julia wanted to say that her husband was not like everyone else, but before she could speak Amadeo said he and Chano had to go somewhere. He motioned to Chano to help him move the trunk to the sidewalk under the awning of a dry goods store and asked the proprietor for a chair for her to sit. Chano bought the boys some pastries and the store owner brought her some cool water and a demitasse of coffee, which she gladly accepted. She had not eaten anything and her empty stomach had made her light-headed. At least she could rest in the proper manner and her children would not be running around in the sun. Later on while they were waiting for Amadeo and Chano to return, the store owner, a Puerto Rican named Eusebio, brought them a pitcher of lemonade and allowed the boys to go into the side yard and play out of the street, which was now filling with wagon traffic.

You will get to like Tampa, Eusebio said to her. When I first got here, longing almost broke my heart. He used the word añoranza for longing, which islanders intone so effectively when referring to their native land. Every moment of every day for three years I had Puerto Rico on my mind. What happened after three years, Julia asked. Curious thing, Eusebio said. One night I went to bed with my heart heavy, my thoughts far away in the hills of my island. When I woke the next morning my añoranza simply lifted and vanished. I don't have a choice but to like it here, Julia said. Yes, you do, the Puerto Rican said. I have known people who give up hope, shut themselves in their houses, and wait to die. Some wait a long time. Look to the future, señora. That is all there is here. The past is on the other side of the moon. Eusebio said that he had come to Tampa because of guavas. Guavas, Julia asked. Yes, he said. The news reached Santurce, where I was living, that there was a lot of guava around here. I had a vision of starting a guava processing plant—paste, marmalade, shells. But when I got to Tampa I discovered there were fewer guava trees here than back home. It was all a rumor the Tampeños started to bring people to their sorry town.

The rumor had spread all over the Caribbean and attracted dreamers of every caste and color to a sleepy mosquito-ridden village of seven hundred souls. There were Dominican farmers, Yucatecan jute workers, Spanish infantrymen, Panamanian musicians, and freed slaves from every corner of the sea alongside the native population they called crackers in those days, lanky Scotch Irishmen and pale-skinned Englishmen who had been driven out of the Confederate states after the war. The people of Tampa sat around staring at each other, wondering how to keep from starving in the desolation and heat of western Florida, when the cigar workers came up from Key West and Cuba in '85 and '86 and built their factories in that part of town they call Ibor City, stress on the *or*. Cigar workers, mostly Cuban, spent their money as if tomorrow the world would end, or as if it never would. They liked good clothes, good houses, good liquor, good women, and good food. Soon all the residents of Tampa were scrambling around trying to satisfy the cigar workers' tastes and unburden them of their freshly earned money. If it were not for the cigar industry, señora, Eusebio told her, Tampa would be a graveyard.

Amadeo and Chano were back when the sun reached its apex and the air was thick and slow, difficult to breathe. The conversation between Julia and the Puerto Rican store owner had long before run itself out and the boys were lying around the porch, swatting flies and trying to doze. Amadeo, sober now, told Julia in a tone much more like himself, to gather up the children. He had found them a house.

Amadeo Terra is thinking. In late afternoon the sun slants through the blinds and the slatted light lands on his face. Then he cannot see the sea or the birds or the motorboats crossing the bay. As the sun descends, the layers of light and shade move across his eyes in a kind of slow agonizing strobe: the brilliant light followed by shadowy relief, followed by burning light. Is he alive or dead? He cannot move, he cannot tell Nurse to move him—he doubts she would oblige. He simply accepts the fact that, unless it rains and the clouds cover the sun, all afternoon he will be subjected to burning light and cooling shade intermittently until night puts a stop to the punishment. At this point Nurse appears with Orderly. They unbuckle him, lift him out of the chair, and put him on the bed. The first time they performed this action many years ago Amadeo was not expecting it and he felt he was lifted into the heavens by two angels; for an instant he abandoned his atheism and rejoiced, but as he waited for a fanfare announcing his entrance into heaven, he descended again and saw their faces (hers strained with the effort of lifting him, his tired and indifferent) as they set him down on the bed. If that is the way angels looked, he was glad he was a nonbeliever. They changed his diaper, fed him his medicines, and tucked him in for the night. He was left alone to sleep or not to sleep, to curse, to ask what he was doing here, was he alive or dead, but no words came out of him, and he understood then, for the first time, that he could not speak. That routine would be repeated, with little variation, every night for the rest of his life until now. Nurse and Orderly turned out not to be angels, not even demons, just people going through the routine of a job, waiting for their shift to be over so they could go home, have a drink, eat dinner, go to sleep. Amadeo's home is the room with the window looking out over the sea, the bed where he sleeps, chair where he sits, day in and day out, in cold and heat, in light and dark, in isolation and unbreachable solitude.

Across the way he hears a woman screaming, Mari, ven acá. Come here, Mariii, followed by a loud wheeze and a fit of coughing and then more screaming. No one comes. No one answers, not even Nurse II, who is probably asleep at her station. The screaming goes on for hours. He would like to yell back to shut her mouth and stick Mari up her ass. Beyond his desperation—he cannot sleep, he cannot respond, he cannot, even if that were his disposition, walk across the hall and say, Madam, Mari is not here. Is there anything I can do for you?—there is a corresponding sense of relief that he is not alone and that, therefore, this is not hell, or a kind of earthly version of it, but purgatory, where souls suffer their cleansing punishments in unison. It is the same sense of relief he feels when he hears Garrido shuffling down the hall in the direction of his door. Garrido peeks his head in and asks, Have you seen my shoelaces? It is always the same question, nothing more. Garrido, who has sunk so deep into his obsession that it has become his personality—there is nothing in this life but his shoelaces—does not realize that Amadeo cannot answer him. Garrido waits a few moments by the door smiling blankly and then moves on. Amadeo can hear his shuffle getting dimmer as he moves away.

And then Amadeo remembers Chinese Lady. She came in the darkness one night two weeks after he arrived at the home. The following night the same thing happened, but the room was not as dark (there may have been a full moon or the blinds of his room may have been left open and the light from the driveway below reflected up through the window) and he could see a small, hunched woman enter his bed, slip under the covers, and speak an incomprehensible gibberish. She was made of toothpicks and skin and he could hear her rustling under the sheets. On the third night, when the light still shone through the blinds, he saw that she had no clothes on. Her hair was short and straight and she had a round face creased with wrinkles. This time, when she started babbling, the language was no different from what he had heard the Chinese people speak in the restaurants of Zanja Street, words that came out flat as pancakes from the mouth and blew up like balloons in midair. He had the urge, excruciating because it was unsatisfied and would always be, to rip off his diaper, turn over on her, and show her the man he really was. Chinese Lady came for many nights and became for Amadeo a welcomed companion who allowed him to tolerate his newly acquired isolation with her talk under the sheets and her tiny curled-up body like a small mammal's providing a warmth he could only imagine. He imagined, too, how she put her hands on him and played with him, all the while speaking in the impenetrable language of the Orient. He cannot imagine any of this now, he can only remember imagining it. One night Chinese Lady stopped coming and her absence was to him as devastating as the knowledge that he would never speak or walk or move again. Chinese Lady in another wing, strapped to her bed so she cannot visit male patients and talk to their bodies? Chinese Lady home taking care of Chinese man and Chinese children? Chinese Lady sparrow singing outside window? Chinese Lady dead? Amadeo Terra feels nothing; he remembers everything.

They walked six blocks into the city away from the port, the two men in front carrying the trunk, Julia behind them with the children. A woman sweeping the sidewalk in front of a store stopped working when they passed, raised her head slowly and stared at them with eyes like sinkholes. Down the street a man with a thick mustache spat behind them and another with his hair disheveled made an evil sign with his hand. That was the welcome: vulgarity and a brutal sun that threatened to consume them. Hey, look, an Andalusian with the thick neck and short arms of a peasant said to his partner as Amadeo and his family passed by. More grist for the mill.

They turned right on the second street and entered a neighborhood in which all the houses looked alike. Rubén the oldest asked how they could tell which was theirs and Chano said by the number. Yours is number 27, a good number, bound to bring luck, and it would be wise for your father to play it as soon as he can. Luck? Amadeo asks. Most of his life he thought he was lucky. Amadeo took Chano's advice, despite his wife's protests, and played the number every week for over twenty years, investing over ten thousand dollars in a venture from which he earned once, when the number hit, a sum of $2,780. In truth, they would not need a number to tell their house from all the others. Theirs was the one apart: ramshackle, abused by the wind and the rain and blanched by the sun. The floorboards on the porch were warped, the front door was off its hinges. Inside was a dank gloom and the smell of animals. It was the house of a leaf stripper, nothing better.

Julia said nothing. She opened the shutters to the front windows and walked past the two small bedrooms to the rear where the kitchen was located. The house was no larger than a country shack, a bohío where peasants squatted. Out in the backyard was an outhouse surrounded by tall weeds. It looked like it had not been used in months. Julia came back to the front room and looked at her husband, but

Amadeo avoided her gaze. He said that they needed to clean things up, pull out the weeds and the cactuses growing around the sides, and get some vegetables growing. There was a bed in the front bedroom and in the living room two broken-down chairs that people called taburetes on the island. The kitchen had a coal stove and a small icebox but there was no space to sit down and eat in a proper manner. Julia said what she had to say by the tense way her hands gripped her skirt and by the tight-lipped silence she had imposed on herself. Her eyebrows arched over her glassy, indignant eyes. Then she surprised him.

We start over, she said.

The three boys stood blankly by her. Their father had pulled them out of bed two nights before and they had gone by oxcart to a place outside the city where they boarded the boat that brought them here. Julia explained vaguely to them that the Spaniards were after their father and they had no choice but to leave everything behind, but it is one thing to hear an explanation and another to understand it. Maybe Rubén sensed that they would not be going back, but he had no idea how close his father had come to having his neck snapped in the garrote chair. For their part the boys saw all of it as an adventure: a trip abroad on a ship, the first of their lives, their arrival in a strange town, bumbling about from street to street, trying to speak a language that turned mealy in their mouths.

Amadeo and Chano stepped outside and Julia could see the two men talking through the front window and could smell the smoke as they lit cigars. She had managed to keep the boys indoors but Rubén the oldest was becoming restless, shadowboxing with an imaginary opponent, while Pastor the middle one was sitting in a corner chewing his collar and looking off into space. From the day he was born she had to work doubly hard to do things for him—tie his shoelaces, wipe his nose, feed him even—that came naturally to the other two. If he ever got rid of that needy look in his eyes, he might be handsome some day, but caught in the cobwebs of his dreaming as he always was, he looked soft and foolish. Only Albertico seemed at ease. He was sitting on the trunk, leaning against his mother's arm, smiling to himself. Julia thought of him as her special one, her gift, who calmed and pacified her. He was the youngest, he was her treat. While the other two were questions, Albertico was an answer.

Just then Amadeo stuck his head inside the door and said that he had to go and would be back soon. Behind him Chano spoke dimly to her that it was a grand pleasure to meet you, señora, and I will stop by soon to see if there is anything you may need. This is a fine town, you will see, señora, the best in all of Florida, he said waiting to kiss her hand again and she burying it deeper in her pocket.

Amadeo Terra can smell himself. He is waiting for Nurse to change him. Sometimes he waits an hour, sometimes two. It used to be she came within minutes of his bowel movement. Now she goes to other patients first, the newer arrivals with relatives who still visit daily and watch over them with hawk eyes. If he could scream he would; if he could move, he would wipe himself. If he could hold it in, that would be best. Nurse enters after a time and gets to work. He follows her with his eyes, but he could just as well close them and imagine the routine. First, she flips off the sheets in one swooping movement, pulls up his robe, undoes the diaper, and folds it up carefully so that none of the mess spills on the mattress. Then she wipes him, moving his testicles out of the way. Useless as they are, they might as well get rid of them like they did his teeth. She puts on a fresh diaper and pulls the robe back down. All the while she is talking baby talk about how much he stinks today and how healthy his poo-poo looks. Poo-poo, that's the term she uses. If he were healthy he wouldn't be here, if he were healthy, he'd be at his bench in the factory, rolling the best clear Havanas in Tampa.

His two surviving sons split the cost for his private room but don't visit. They are waiting for him to die so they won't have to pay any more to keep this piece of meat their father has become out of the way. They think his brain is as dead as the rest of him, but Amadeo knows it is sharper than it ever was, less cluttered with the daily demands they and their mother placed on him. He can remember things, he can think. He can compute, for example, the total amount of money he earned in his life: $1,400,000 and change. The week before he added up the number of cigars he rolled and the week before that the number of times he had sex. What would his sons think of that? Pastor married an American and went off to the northern suburbs. Rubén is a worthless poet in New York. Neither has visited him in years.

At first it was different. Even if they thought of their father as so much brainless matter, they came to the home and tried to distract him with talk of their lives. Rubén discussed poetry and recited some of his poems out loud to his father. Amadeo didn't understand them and wished he could speak so he could tell Rubén he was wasting his time; he would never be as good as Martí. Pastor, the middle one, is married to a leggy blond from Ohio who used to bring him peach pies he couldn't eat because they made him gag. He has a daughter, who is studying to be a doctor. She visited only once and taught Amadeo to speak with his eyes. One blink means yes, two means no. Three blinks means thirst, four means hunger. Five means pain, which is meaningless since pain is not something he can feel in his condition. Six is doctor. Seven is change me. Eight and nine he forgets and ten means help, but no one in Santa Gertrudis has had the patience to wait for him to blink ten times, and so he does not even try. All the thinking has made him drool but Nurse is uninterested in wiping him. If you want to make a mess of yourself, go right ahead, she says. You should be ashamed, acting like a silly baby. A grown man, she says, and leaves.

Amadeo is alone again. He can think without interruption, he can remember what he did and what he did not do. Sometimes he remembers things as they actually happened; other times he changes them. He doesn't care anymore what is true and what is not, if he sees events now as they happened then. No one is listening. No one is here to correct him. If he is an elephant on Monday, so be it. If he is an insect on Tuesday, who is there to tell him he is not? He can drool, he can shit again, he can be a killer of men, a seducer of women, he can be an old man lying helpless in bed entertaining himself with stories. He can remember the time he spent seeking his fortune, making the money that is the real measure of a man, his first job sweeping the cigar factory floor in Pinar del Río. He can remember learning by watching the rollers in their benches, silently, never asking any questions because they would give the wrong answer just to throw him off. Cigar rollers are like that. He took tobacco home, practiced through the day and night until he could roll a perfecto with his eyes closed. He remembers moving to Elpidio's house, Elpidio with his caramel skin and green eyes who taught him the shape, the spirit of the cigar, without which it is simply a bunch of rolled tobacco like the Indians used to make. Amadeo became a stripper and made sorter in a year. No one had ever risen so fast in the factories of Pinar del Río. Still, they refused to give him a bench. So he worked for Elpidio who ran a chinchal, what they call a buckeye in el Norte, from the house. The time came when Amadeo didn't need the miserable salary they paid him at the factory. If he stayed it was because he got his tobacco for free. In those days it was considered beneath the rollers' dignity to have their allotment of tobacco weighed at the beginning and end of each day as happened later after the weight-scale strike. Whatever was left over was there for anyone to take, and Amadeo took what he needed. War broke out in 1868 in Oriente and soon spread to Pinar del Río. Amadeo's father, a Canary Islander with the disposition of a mule, thought his son would run off with the rebels at the first opportunity, and so, the next year he sent

Amadeo to Campeche, where a cousin of his owned a hemp factory. Amadeo remembers his father putting him on an oxcart with a family of six who were escaping the ravages of war for the relative safety of Havana. The head of the family, a tobacco farmer from San Juan y Martínez, told Amadeo that he had just had his farm burned by a column of voluntarios. The family had been assigned for reconcentration but escaped the voluntarios and were now headed for the capital where he hoped they would be safe. This hope was not shared by the others and Amadeo re-members now the drawn look of fear on the faces of the women, coupled with resignation and a several-days-old hunger. Amadeo remembers, too, the dim look on his own mother's face as they parted—she was never an affection-ate woman—and the weak wave of her hand as he climbed on the cart.

For a week they lumbered through the countryside, traveling east after the sun went down to avoid detection by the warring factions. With him Amadeo had brought a sack of food his mother prepared containing several cans of sardines, hard-boiled eggs, lard crackers and a bottle of well water, which he shared with the farmer's family until the provisions ran out. He went hungry for the first time in his life. He saw the faces of the dead, lying contorted on the ground or hanging from the trees. Not one of them was smiling or at peace or happy or sad. All of them were vacant, graceless, drained. They drove past a small child abandoned on the road and when one of the women asked the driver to stop, he said, if he's got the fare he can get on, if not, he can wait for the next driver. As they moved on, Amadeo threw his last cracker in the boy's direction. The cart reached Havana three days later, an hour before the ship sailed for Yucatán. The captain, an old friend of his father, it turned out, had to bribe a harbor official who claimed Amadeo's papers were not in order.

Amadeo was in Campeche two years, long enough to buy his way back to Cuba to confront his father for having sent him away, but by then the old man had died. When he got to the house there was only his mother, silent and inscrutable, slowly dying of malnutrition. The interminable war was raging and there was little food to be had in the provinces. Mamá, he said, I'm home. But it was like speaking to a stone. He went out and bought a loaf of stale bread and tried to have her eat it. When she finally opened her mouth such a pestilential odor came out that he was revolted and had to turn his face away. He tried to find a doctor for her that day and the next but the three that he spoke to wanted more money than he had. He even went as far as threatening the last one, who pulled a pistol from inside his coat and put it right between Amadeo's eyes. The doctor pulled the trigger but the gun jammed, then he quickly slammed the door and locked it behind him and Amadeo was left standing on the porch, urine dripping from his pant cuffs onto the imported Italian tiles. Amadeo's mother survived the war and the starvation as she had survived all the misfortunes in her life, by waiting them out. Ten years later, nearly blind from cataracts, she met her fate under the wheels of a fruit vendor's wagon.

Amadeo senses that his body is drying out and turning to dust. His instinct is to raise his head and look for himself but, of course, he cannot do this. He lowers his eyes as far as they will go. All he sees is the mound of his body covered by white sheets, underneath which, he is certain, his extremities, his torso, his organs and his bones are slowly becoming dust. He can feel it floating over the bed in pink and yellow layers. Is this how death comes, in a dissolution of the corporeal self, in a desiccation of fluids and dispersion of matter into the air? Nurse enters with her clinking jars of baby food and her empty disposition. Amadeo closes his eyes, makes believe he is still asleep. Mr. Terra, wake up, Mr. Terra. She has put the tray on the rolling table and is pulling the sheet off him. In one swooping motion it flies up like a sail catching wind and dispels the clouds that have risen from him. She moves him this way and that, wipes him with a wet towel, puts on a fresh diaper, pulls down his robe, and cranks up the bed so she can feed him. This time there is no mango, but he is unwilling to fight her and so he opens his mouth willingly and lets her spoon into him whatever she has brought. Nothing he recognizes. In two minutes she is done and congratulates him on his cooperation. She wipes his face, gathers the tray and leaves. Amadeo cannot think of anything just then. Something is happening inside his body he doesn't like, groups of people gathering on street corners, in parks, upset at some political unfairness, a stolen election, a breakdown of the system. More people gather and the outrage grows, followed by a rallying cry. The crowd spills onto the streets. A boy throws a Molotov cocktail at a police wagon; someone else sets fire to a mound of refuse. Leaders materialize out of nowhere. Now the mob is running down the streets of the city breaking windows, throwing rocks, screaming. Old men are trampled, baby trams upended. Amadeo can feel it in his body. There is a volley of shots from a contingent of army regulars who block the boulevard. Several young men fall. The people are angry and blind with rage, Death to the Spaniards, Death to the King, ¡Viva Cuba! Amadeo opens his mouth to scream for help and a fierce jet of food shoots out and lands on the white snow of his belly. He closes his eyes, exhausted. He can feel his heavy breathing, his heartbeat in his ears, the curfew siren sounding, the random shots, the black smoke rising from buildings torched by the mob, the grave-like quiet of the streets broken only by the sound of waves washing up on shore.

Sometimes you fall in with a woman and there is nothing you can do. Your brain says here and that's where you stop to tie up your mule, convince yourself that she's the one and you marry her. She may not be the most beautiful or the best housekeeper or the hottest in bed. No matter. You dismiss the superlatives. And so it was with Julia. She understood him and she knew what it meant to be a cigar maker, as good as could be found on the island. And she had character. She learned when to stay out of his way and when to stand up to him. She grew to know, as if she was clairvoyant, when his moods were about to strike before he did. One month he would take up gambling and lose two, three thousand pesos at the cockfights. Two months later he would go on a drinking binge that lasted three days and come home broken and helpless. She would be waiting for him with a plate of rice and vaca frita. Despite what he told himself then, it occurs to him that

Julia was never wrathful but mistress of a silence that carried all she could ever say to him. The silence became intolerable and he filled it with his guilt. Julia never spoke about her unhappiness because she had no time for it. For him only tobacco brought happiness.

Even now, he thinks, if he could get his hands on some leaf, a chaveta, a rolling bench, he could do it, and he imagines himself spreading out the binder leaf on the table, taking some filler in his left hand and shaping it not too tightly, not too loosely, then placing the filler on the binder and wrapping it, working it to the right shape. When he is done with that, he gets to the most delicate part of the operation. He takes the moist wrapper leaf and stretches it out on the bench as far as it will go without splitting, so thin it is almost transparent; he puts the bound filler on the wrapper and starts to wrap quickly and carefully at an angle, cutting excess as he goes and keeping the left hand rolling, always rolling, carving a half moon on the final strip to cover the tip. After many years of practice he can roll as he breathes, with an instinctive economy and delicacy of movement. His hands are angels, his hands are sparrows, spiders, arañas tabaqueras. Just then Nurse enters and makes a mock-horrified face at all the half-digested food on his stomach. Mr. Terra, Mr. Terra, what am I going to do with you? A cigar maker has nothing if not his hands and a clear mind. The reason for the hands is obvious. The clear mind he needs in order to keep his independence and know his friends from his enemies. Mr. Terra, I am tired of having to change you every few hours. You make me work double time. They don't pay me enough, Mr. Terra. He could have followed Julia back, he could have left everything behind once again, and started over in Havana, the city he loved, but by then he had Amalia. He thought he loved her more, he thought he had at last found the woman he needed, but she was just young and eager. Julia was old and tired, dried out with work and grief after the death of Albertico. Amalia was plump and full and moved like a filly. She was a lake in bed, she was snake and seal and storm and swamp, she was a cloud on fire. Julia went and he stayed behind and then she died. Nurse has pushed his body to the side so that she can pull off the soiled bedding. With his face buried in the pillow he cannot breathe and tries to get her attention by blinking several times. He sucks air in through his mouth but all that enters is the pillow cover, he is breathing cotton, he feels the world blackening and then, for the first time in almost five years, a sound comes out of him, between a groan and a scream. Nurse rushes to the side of the bed and pulls him back into light and air. His eyes are burning, his head is about to explode, but he can breathe. Nurse holds his head with both her hands.

Mr. Terra, Mr. Terra, are you all right, she says out of breath herself. Mr. Terra, she is rubbing his chin, lifting his head, Mr. Terra, are you all right? Julia, his mind is stuck on Julia. Mr. Terra, your eyes. More food comes, but this time it oozes out of him and flows down his cheek. Mr. Terra, Mr. Terra. Julia, he remembers her steady eyes, her small strong hands, the curve of her neck, her thick black hair. He can do nothing but remember, the cloud of dust floating over his bed, settling on the sheets. Nurse is frantic. She rushes out of the room and for a few minutes Amadeo is alone. In his imagination he is not afraid, but his mind is firing. He remembers the first time he saw Julia in her father's bodega, standing behind the counter, slight and diaphanous. He bought what they had: five pounds of bacalao, three pounds of beans, ten pounds of cornmeal. Their first kiss was behind her parents' garden. He was walking her home from the store. He grabbed her by the arm and stopped her. He said her name and put his lips awkwardly on hers. What, she said pulling away softly and smiling. He tried to kiss her again but she turned her face. What, she asked again. He was eighteen. She was fifteen.

He had a daughter with Amalia—Alina, dark-skinned like her mother, with eyes like caimito pits. On Sundays her mother would dress her in white Indian lace and he would take her to the park to show her off in front of his friends, who envied him because he had a beautiful young woman and a daughter like a dark pearl. Then Aurelio Menéndez, the Galician, emboldened by an afternoon of rum, told him in the park that Amalia was a whore who bedded down the first fool who came along. Amadeo took Alina home and came back with his chaveta and attacked Aurelio with such fierceness that strips of flesh were hanging from his face like tobacco leaves from their stalk. After Aurelio came back from the hospital they took to calling him crucigrama because the scars on his face looked like a crossword puzzle. Still, Aurelio's comment put doubts in Amadeo's head and those doubts corroded his love. A vision came to him of Amalia braying like a donkey while she was being ridden by the neighborhood barber. No matter what he tried Amadeo could not rid himself of the vision and the reasonable part of him, the one that insisted that Amalia loved him faithfully and would never be with another man, let alone the neighborhood barber, was eventually drowned out. He took to leaving work early, bringing his chaveta with him, fully expecting to catch them in flagrante delicto. He told Amalia he was going on a trip and instead took a room on the other side of town and would show up in the neighborhood disguised as a street sweeper or a knife sharpener. He saw nothing that would confirm his suspicions. The vision, rather than disappearing altogether, actually gained in intensity and mutated into different scenes. He saw her with two men, one white, one black; he saw her with another woman (this was not so bad); he saw her with a dog. He couldn't sleep; he lost weight. Finally, in a crescendo of outrage, he saw her with Aurelio Menéndez and his crossword-puzzle face, twisted together in bed, groaning and screaming and making such a scandal that the neighborhood boys came to the window to watch. It was as if someone had put a curse on him. Years later he would learn that someone had, but at the time he didn't believe in curses and so he dismissed that possibility as an invention of his confused mind. In desperation he gathered some of his things and took two thousand pesos he had hidden under a loose tile in the kitchen. Amalia threw herself on him, pleading and begging for him not to leave, but all he saw before him was a whoring witch smeared with other men's semen. He went to the port and bought a one-way ticket on a steamer headed for Panama. There he walked the streets a few weeks, cleansing himself of the poison that had infected him, and eventually found work in a cigar factory. Tobacco was his salvation. He made enough money to buy a sawmill and two houses, but he knew the moment he got off the ship that Colón was not a place where he would stay. It was a poor sad city with too many men waiting out their misery. During those four years all his thoughts were on his daughter Alina, whom he would never see again, and her mother, who bore the brunt of his madness, but above all he thought of Julia, who'd been everything to him.

Amadeo opens his eyes and sees Orderly bent over the bed bathing him. He sees his naked belly like a deflated sack of lard, falling off to the side. The skin on it is pale and veiny and it has lost most of the hair that once covered it. Orderly moves a sponge down each of his legs and as he does so Amadeo's belly wobbles. Amadeo thinks the body on the bed is no longer his. The flesh and bone are still attached to the neck, but no matter how strongly he wills it, he cannot make his body move. It surprises him that after all these years he still tries. Amadeo Terra is trying. Amadeo Terra is alive and he becomes elated at the thought. The excitement leads him to press his lips together and start drooling. Orderly sees him and calls him a crazy cat spitting all over, making a mess of himself as if he weren't already in a bad enough situation. Amadeo wants to tell him to go to hell, negro de mierda, but all that comes out of him is more drool, a river of drool sliding out of his tight mouth, running down his chin to the layers of fat around his neck. He wants to drown Orderly with his spit and so much does come out that Orderly is frozen in astonishment. A stream of saliva is spreading out from Amadeo's chin and wetting the fresh sheets Orderly has just covered him with. For a moment Orderly looks worried, then angry, and he calls Amadeo a sorry-ass motherfucker as he stomps out of the room. Soon thereafter Nurse appears followed by Orderly. Amadeo looks at her apologetically but it does no good. Nurse gives a speech about how he should behave himself, acting like that in front of Orderly and scaring the bejesus (that is the word she uses) out of him. As punishment, she says, we are not going to change your sheets anymore today. You can lie there in your filth. Amadeo Terra is smiling to himself. He feels strong and radiant, as if he had just won a great battle, but what Nurse and Orderly see is the expressionless look of a vegetable.

oday is the day of the nuns. A small one Amadeo
has never seen before enters the room. Her name,
she says, is Sor Diminuta. She is dressed in a brown
habit made of uncombed cotton that hangs loosely over a
long-sleeved white shirt. It is impossible for Amadeo to
guess her age, but her hands, wrinkled and veined, are not
a young woman's. Her hair is hidden by a white band around
her forehead and over it the veil of her order. She has a tri-
angular face splotched with red as if she had been out in the
sun too long. From her neck hangs a large silver crucifix,
her only adornment besides the wedding band on the left
hand. Sor Diminuta begins with a prayer to St. Albenius,

the patron saint of the ill and those about to die. Amadeo listens to the nun's dreamy voice but it is difficult for him to follow the words. Like all the prayers he has heard during his lifetime, hers is mind-numbing and he lets his thoughts wander to the most recondite places of his memory, where he finds fragments of his previous life— a face, a view of the sea from a deserted beach, the street in front of his house, the jewelry box where his father kept his billfold and watch. St. Albenius, you who have interceded on behalf of so many unfortunate and suffering servants of Our Lord, raise your voice to him on Amadeo's behalf, who calls to you humbly in his hour of greatest need. Who was this Saint Albenius who had God's ear? What martyrdom did he suffer? Amadeo observes Sor Diminuta from his bed and notices that she has her eyes closed and hands open upward in supplication. She looks like a sparrow about to take flight. The jewelry box: It was made of a dark wood, rectangular with scalloped edges, and on the cover there was an etching of a map of the world. Every afternoon when he arrived home from the fields or the store, his father emptied his pockets. First, the loose change, then the scraps of paper with the names of people he talked to that day, then the gold key chain. He unclasped it from his vest and pulled the chain up as if it were a fish line heavy with a fresh catch until the bunch of little fishes came out of his pocket and dangled before Amadeo's eyes. It hung there for a moment before descending into the confines of the jewelry box.

Sor Diminuta is about to finish her prayer. He can tell by the way her voice has reached a crescendo and entered another register. She is standing over the bed and her eyelids, suspended halfway down the balls of her eyes, are fluttering. We exhort you to bring Christ Our Lord this request that your faithful servant Amadeo Terra and all of the sick and dying who surround us may be touched by the grace of the Holy Spirit, amen. As she ends the oration she lets out a deep breath and smiles down at Amadeo, exposing a set of large stained teeth. Sor Diminuta then takes out a brush from the pocket of her habit and begins to brush his hair, pushing back with her free hand the longer strands on the sides of his scalp. She takes her time and although he cannot feel her hands, he knows they are delicate and soft. He imagines them moving against his ears and the top of his forehead. He looks down and notices that the crucifix suspended from her neck is resting on his chest, and he remembers how it would unsettle him to have Julia's crucifix dangle over him while they made love. Take it off, he said one night. She refused, claiming she had made a vow to the Virgin of Charity not to take it off until the day of her death. He threatened reprisals. She did not say anything in response but put on an ankle-length nightgown, got in bed, and turned her back to him. For a month the Terra household was celibate. Every night Amadeo commanded her to get rid of the thing, it meant nothing anyway, and every night Julia stormed out of the bedroom and sat on the front porch reciting the rosary until sex was the farthest thing from her mind. On the thirtieth day, when Amadeo was contemplating visiting one of the bordellos on the other side of the city to relieve himself, Julia approached him in the living room and said I will not take it off but I will wear it down my back. Amadeo consented and the standoff was broken. In time the crucifix found its way back to the front, but by then Amadeo had accepted the fact that Christ would be forever between them in bed.

When she is finished combing the strands of white hair that are still left on his scalp, Sor Diminuta leans over him to arrange the pillows around his head. She doesn't know—how could she?—that he does not feel any more comfortable or uncomfortable than before, that it does not matter whether his head is this way or that. He can smell the strong ascetic odor of her unwashed body through the heavy fabric of her habit. Acrid and penetrating, it is not a pleasant smell but it makes him think of women he has known and how they smelled of raw milk or incense or the bottom of a well or the sea or a wild mare. Some smelled like castile soap, others like a sugarcane field after rain. One smelled like an outhouse, another like tar, a third like the sulfur of hell. Many smelled like garlic. Many more smelled like flowers. At least two smelled like his mother. He catches himself getting worked up over an odorous nun and waits for her to finish accommodating him. She smiles her crooked smile again and Amadeo blinks in recognition. She sits down next to the head of the bed on the chair where Nurse sits to feed him and begins to recite a rosary, whispering each prayer softly, rocking back and forth surrounded by the mist of an intolerable monotony. He sees the beads passing through her fingers and the susurrus of Aves broken by the occasional Pater Noster. Sitting away from him Sor Diminuta smells more like ripe hay ready for harvesting, like those fields he passed in the Catskills in the early fall once years ago. Beautiful country. He could have moved up there to do union work in Albany, but Tampa was the farthest north Julia was willing to go. Up north Sor Diminuta can go days without bathing and no one will notice. People will pass by her on the street and think she is just another nun on her way to vespers. They will say, Good afternoon, Sister, and never imagine the irresistible scent of a wild she-wolf that lurks within the folds of her habit. Here in this heat is another matter, and

Amadeo is surprised her mother superior has not discussed with her the sanctifying properties of bathing.

Julia's scent, on the other hand, changed throughout the day. In the morning after waking she smelled like a beach. When stoking the stove for dinner she smelled like coal smoke and when cooking she smelled like beans or ajiaco or stewed pigs' feet. He'd keep his distance then. He can see her through the steam: hair tied back, a few strands of it loose, and her eyes looking down at the pot with the concentration of an alchemist. Sometimes she smelled like oranges, other times like clove. When her elbow hurt she smelled like iguana oil, which she claimed cured her arthritis, and when plucking chickens, well, he didn't want to think about that. At night after her bath Julia gave off the scent of a field of flowers, or what he imagined to be a field of flowers since he'd never been in one, and in bed naked, she smelled like desire itself. Then, one afternoon while he was rummaging through a kitchen cabinet in search of a sharpener for his chaveta, he found a bottle of lilac water. He opened the bottle and was surprised to find Julia's odor wafting out. This happened several days into one of the strikes at the factory. When he confronted her with the fact that she was wasting their money on frivolous things, she responded that it was her prerogative to smell however she wanted, and she wanted to smell like a lady, not a street cleaner. The strike could last a long time, he said. It was a gift, she said. Her statement caught him by surprise and with his mind occupied by union matters, he dropped the subject. The question he did not ask, however, remained in his mind like a splinter that made its presence felt whenever he was about to embark on one of his escapades. Why would she hide the bottle? The conclusion he reached, that the intentions of the giver were far from innocent and that she had somehow encouraged his behavior, angered him at times, but he kept from saying anything out of a sense that it would reveal a weakness for her he would just as soon keep hidden. What if her loyalty was not as absolute as he had once assumed? What would he do? Years later, when their marriage was dying, he learned that Julia had been receiving a monthly bottle of cologne from a destitute poet who had been her paramour in Havana before Amadeo had come upon her at her father's store and changed the course of her life. It is a good thing I did not learn about the poet then, he said to her. I would have choked the poor fellow to death. He was a nice man, she said. The world is full of nice men, Amadeo said lying back on his chair. Julia waited a few moments before adding that the poet had died of tuberculosis. A fitting death, Amadeo said. He died in the hospital without anyone to keep him company. All the better. They buried him in a potter's field. A perfect poet's death, he said then asked her how she knew all this. His mother wrote to me. You knew his mother? The whole family. We were going to be married. You were going to marry a poet? How quaint, Amadeo said. He can remember the conversation as clearly as he can smell the nun. When was the last time you received a bottle of cologne from him? Two years ago. But you still smell of lilacs. How can that be? His mother sends me the cologne now. Lilacs are my favorite flowers. What do poets know about flowers, he thinks with the drone of Sor Diminuta's prayers in the background. When the strike was over Amadeo started buying Julia lilac water on a regular basis. The poet died as a poet should, poor, forlorn, and consumptive. No big loss, he thought. Cuba is cursed with too many poets and too many queers and the women who pamper them.

Nurse comes in bearing the food tray followed by Orderly. Sor Diminuta intercepts her as she is about to place the tray on the rolling table and volunteers to feed him. Nurse gladly obliges but first they have to put him into the chair. He doesn't weigh as much as you think, Nurse offers by way of comment. Amadeo sees the ceiling suddenly get near, then far again, and hears his body flop softly onto the plastic chair. Orderly quickly ties him up and places a paper bib on his chest before following Nurse out of the room. Sor Diminuta rearranges Amadeo's shoulders and head and rolls the table next to the chair. Her smell is approaching again but he is much more interested in reading the baby food labels. If she gives him mango he will rise from his bed, he will shout out, he will get an erection the size of Florida. But it is not mango. Her holy woman's hand drops the anonymous pastes carefully into his mouth. One is earthy and gray like liver; the other is airy like apricot. Sor Diminuta is smiling all the while. He is docile, opening his mouth as far as it goes for each spoonful. Once he swallows too quickly and chokes, spitting the paste back up. The nun wipes his chin and keeps smiling. He smiles back or imagines smiling back and is overcome. There is goodness in her eyes, and in her lips, full and moist over bad teeth, a hint of past sensuality. Are you enjoying yourself, Sor Diminuta? Yes, Mr. Terra, and so are you. Have you ever had a man? Yes, Mr. Terra, I have Christ. Leave Christ out of this. I don't need any other men. Tell me you love men, tell me you love me. But she is saying something else, she is trying to settle him down, then he notices he has choked again and spit up more of the paste onto his chin and neck. She is rubbing his temples and he feels like heaven and hell combined. Do you shave your armpits, Sor Diminuta? Do you bleed on your underwear, do you scratch your itch? He takes a deep breath and it smells like God, the Devil, all the angels singing off key and the damned ones grunting like pigs. He opens his eyes, he closes them. Imagining her touch brings a calm like the sun rising over palm trees.

When Amadeo awakens Sor Diminuta is gone. The late afternoon light is streaking in through the blinds once again and hitting him squarely in the face. This time he tries to occupy himself by looking around the room. On the corner where the window meets the wall, about half-way up, he sees a black spot he has not noticed before. The glare makes him close his eyes and when he opens them again, the spot has moved farther to the left away from the corner. He focuses on it to see if it is alive or simply a smudge of dirt distorted by the sunlight on his face. Just as he is about to make out its shape, the thing scurries up to the left, then laterally to the right and stops in a spot of wall out of the light. A spider is not a creature he can tolerate, a spider leaves blank places in his reasoning that he can only fill with more spiders, hundreds of them, crawling over and under each other. They move down the wall and scamper across the floor, five hundred sets of legs scratching the linoleum, jaws clacking together until all other noises are drowned out. A pungent oily smell suffuses the room. The spiders reach Amadeo's chair and start climbing up the sides. Some fall off but many more take their place, clinging to the varnished wood of the legs and the plastic of the armrests. He tries to tell himself that his imagination is confusing past with present, memory and reality but by the time the first spider crawls onto the horizontal plane of the seat, Amadeo is six years old and has just awakened to find the creatures are everywhere on his lap and arms, their hairy legs and beady eyes moving toward his face. He is paralyzed with fear and the spiders, tiny newly hatched tarantulas are on his cheeks now, scratching his nostrils, crawling into the folds of his ears. He can hear the humming sounds they make to communicate among themselves, the small ones sliding over his forehead, tangled in the thicket of his hair. Then a wave of water falls on him and his mother's face appears illumined by kerosene light. His father is behind her holding a metal bucket. She rushes over to Amadeo and begins brushing spiders off his body. He can breathe now and he is shivering from the cold water his father has thrown at him but he will not cry. Why not, he wonders now. Because his father is there and Amadeo will not cry in front of his father, no matter how much fear is in him. As his mother is drying him with a towel, his father is slapping at the spiders on the bed with a broom and crushing them under his heel on the floor. Later, when his fear turns to disgust, Amadeo vows to himself he will kill every spider he comes across. They become his enemies. His hatred of them will be embodied in the act of extermination he will perform with a machine-like efficiency for the rest of his life. The spider, small, innocuous on the beige surface, is moving toward the door. Amadeo remembers back to the thousands of spiders he has flattened under his heel, crushed under rocks, buried in sand, sprayed with insecticide, or bathed in gasoline and torched. This one strolling across the wall of his room will get away.

Time falls into a deep well. He hears a splash, sees the water turn into his friend Chano's face, doomed, moon-smeared. He smells the dampness rising, the moss on the stones, Chano floating between the darkness and the light, his clothes in tatters, his skin bloated and blue. The practice in those days was to have lectores, or readers, distract the cigar rollers by reading to them. Lectores were men of great learning and polish and Chano wanted very much to be one of them. He used to wait outside the factory door hoping the workers would one day hire him to read, but they always picked one of the more established readers from Havana or Key West. The more this happened, the more flamboyant Chano became, dressing up in outrageous costumes, accentuating his s's and trilling his r's and otherwise carrying on like a clown, hoping to stand out from all the others vying to sit at the reader's platform. The workers coming into the factory said, Payaso, who let you out of the circus, but Chano waved off the insults and persisted until one day when the regular lector failed to show, and he was granted an audition. Chano was ready. As his text he chose a selection from Pérez Galdós's *Juan Martín el empecinado* that describes the manner in which the Spaniards met the invading Napoleonic forces, and he declaimed it from memory with such skill and eloquence that the workers did what they had never done before: they stopped their rolling, stood in place, and gave Chano a rousing applause. At that moment Chano went from being a fool to being a lector, which is how Amadeo met him, a flamboyant but respected member of his profession. Amadeo never learned exactly why he died, but he knew Chano was involved in some unsavory deals with the Sicilians on Fourteenth Street— prostitution and bolita, mostly. It was common knowledge that the Sicilians wanted control, but Chano was intent on standing his ground. They cut his throat and threw him down a well. Amadeo was present when they pulled up the body.

What do Nurse and Orderly and Sor Diminuta and Nurse II and Physical Therapist know about him? There is information in his file about his condition, his age, weight, blood pressure, marital status, his sons' addresses and phone numbers (his sons wait for those phones to ring with the ultimate news). There is even a statement about his profession but no indication as to what that means: the time he spent perfecting his art, the hours and days rolling, the years at the table. Do they know the satisfaction of holding a cigar you made yourself, perfectly shaped and sized, that a man will smoke and draw deep pleasure from? Do they know what he thinks about as he lies in bed waiting for them to come and relieve him of his solitude? All they see is a large piece of breathing flesh that must be changed twice a day, fed three times, moved in and out of the bed and kept in minimal working order until such time as the mechanism fails conclusively and there is nothing else to do but carry the worthless hunk of meat out of here, notify the family and get the bed ready for the next patient. There is a long waiting list to join this club.

If he had a mirror what would he see? He would see a face as flat as a cartoon, he would see the eyes inflamed with the past, he would see no future, he would see faint eyebrows where before there were thick bushes, he would see pale skin and thin veins spreading under his cheeks like blue rivers, blue canals in a distant planet, he would see the eyes of a toad, green, then brown, then bleared with time, then straining sideways to keep watch of the dark shadow that refuses to leave his bedside, in that shadow almost a smile, almost a dance in and out of the mirror's frame, he would see a mockingbird on a fence post, flicking its tail up and down, up and down, before flying off into memory, he would see his sunken lips turned downward like a general who has just sent his army to certain defeat, he will see fate, he will see fear, he will see a nose that has lost its shape, sharp bone cutting air, he will see the smoke of the incense of his wistfulness, he will see what he did not do, he will see money turning into leafmeal, he will see the broken body of his son, he will feel his throat throttled by grief, by guilt, soft creases in the temple where the blood has pulsed, he will see the scarred face of the man he mutilated, of the men he should have killed but thought the better of it, he will see a chin where the stubble of white beard is growing, he will not see his tongue, he will not see his body, he will see the mole on his forehead over the left eyebrow, touch of the woman, his wife would say, hair tousled, thinned out over the dome of his skull, he will see anguish and peace fighting a battle to the death, pride crumbling like a chimney, a broom sweeping a wood floor, the hands holding the broom, he will see the dry bed of his intelligence, the garden of his love beginning to blossom, many struggles with others but many more with himself, he will see the crud of his body, he will see his wife, her closed and dreaming eyes, he will see that it is not the money or the women or the houses, he will see clouds, a field of grass, he wishes he could see his island, a storm gathering over the sea, water pooling into puddles, he will see the aftermath of battle, piled bodies, burning trees, torn clothes, hungry men, he will see the happy fool of his brother Tavito who was always in love, he will see an empty mirror, end of the straight line, end of the self.

He has been dying a long time, longer than they all thought possible—the doctors, the nurses, his sons with the quizzical stares and their hands on their wallets. They come to him when he least expects, taking him back, moving him forward, peering into his eyes and wondering what is left inside. Where is the switch he can throw to make those faces disappear, silence their voices? When he first came to Santa Gertrudis they removed all the mirrors out of his room and put up pictures instead: a teary clown, a vase of lime-colored flowers, a mountainscape that does not resemble any mountains he has ever seen. The clown is warping, the flowers are drooping, the snow on the mountains has yellowed. He remembers a child's picture of a horse done in crayon. The horse is red with a green tail and yellow nostrils. A cowboy dressed in black has just gotten off the horse and points the gun at the white sky where a bird is flying. He can't remember which of his sons drew the picture or if he himself did or if he is just now making it up. He remembers one of a mother holding a staff, of a bishop leering. Best of all, he remembers a naked woman reclining on a couch. Her hands, folded behind her head, are hidden by thick curly hair. She is not afraid to show her body—her armpits, her perfect breasts, the line of down from her navel to her pubis—and she looks brazenly out at the man beyond the frame. She lets him know that she could, momentarily, rise from the couch, get dressed, leave the room, as easily as she could take him in her arms.

Sometimes his memory is animated, a scene or event he is a part of, a door has opened in his chest and he walks through. This kind of memory has a dreamlike quality. For example, he is now standing with Julia on the porch of his Ibor house watching a group of men heading toward his house. At the head are Julio Mendoza and Obdulio Brito and behind them is Chano, talking with a smaller man next to him. The small man walks as if he were floating over the ground, turning his head and nodding in response to someone's comment or grabbing another man's arm in solidarity. Look, Amadeo says to Julia, Martí is coming to our house. Julia recognizes all the familiar faces and in their midst the small man, looking very much like photogravures she has seen—the thick mustache hiding his mouth, the broad forehead, the deep determined eyes, the look of a man who knows he will die soon, the look of a poet. She is surprised how frail he seems—a strong breeze could pick him up and send him flying. Julia leans on her husband and grabs his arm. Why, she asks. I don't know, he says. Perhaps he needs a quiet place to rest. The group stops in front of the porch and Chano introduces Martí to Amadeo and Julia. The poet is poorly dressed in a wrinkled black suit. His fingers are slender and delicate, still bearing the ink stains of that morning's work. Martí shakes hands with Amadeo then turns his attention to Julia. He takes her hand in his and brings it to his lips. Pase usted, Señor Martí, she says after waiting a moment for her husband to speak. Dígame Pepe, por favor, he says, que aquí todos somos cubanos, as if being Cuban puts them all on the same plane. Julia smiles and allows herself to respond, Pero usted es el más cubano de todos, the most Cuban of all, a statement that everyone likes and reaches Martí's pride, for he straightens his shoulders and his face broadens with a smile. What does it mean to be Cuban, Amadeo thinks. It is not a question he has spent much time pondering. Sometimes it comes from inside, a place that no one can change or alter. Sometimes it comes from the way he responds to a woman walking past or an urge for coffee, a cigar, a joke. Sometimes he will hear Spanish spoken a certain way or listen to music when Nurse II turns the radio to the Spanish-language station. Once they played an old bolero and he thought his heart would burst out of his chest with longing—añoranza—for his native land and his people. His people, he still thinks of them that way. Mostly in Santa Gertrudis he is not Cuban, no matter how much he wants to be—he is alive, that's all, devoid of the things that make him one way or another. But Amadeo is remembering that most Cuban of men sitting in his living room in a most un-Cuban way: quiet and withdrawn while the other men argue and gesticulate and try to impress each other with their political fervor. When Julia approaches Martí with a demitasse of coffee, the poet awakens from his mood and his face lightens. Amadeo notices that his hand lingers under hers as she passes him the cup and that his wife seems pleased by this. Then Martí sits back on the chair, lost in the labyrinth of his thought. It is an image that has stayed in Amadeo's mind until the present day—the poet ruminating—and he has never been sure if it was a mere pose or if that is the way poets are. What does Amadeo know about poets? Nothing, except that they spend a lot of time thinking, like his son Rubén in New York.

Later that day Martí would give an impromptu speech in front of the Martínez Ibor factory urging all Tampa Cubans to support the cause. Among those listening was Rubén, who was so inspired that he followed the poet to New York and waited for the invasion of the island to materialize. By the time the war finally erupted in 1895 and Martí sailed for Cuba, Rubén had forgotten all about his patriotism and was himself engaged in the thankless pursuit of trying to be a poet in a city that breeds poets only to devour them before they reach maturity. His mother tried to steer him away from a life of misery with fervent letters about the dangers of the big city and the difficulties of a poet's life, which she knew all too well. When that didn't work she pleaded with him that he was staining the family honor (what honor, he had asked her in one of his rare letters home, and received no answer). In Amadeo's mind Rubén was a worthless fool. He is following in Martí's footsteps, Julia told her husband. A real man makes his own footsteps, Amadeo said through his cigar. He is a dreamer, she said. At his age I was working sixty hours a week. He is our son. Don't be so hard. Amadeo did not respond. He took in the smoke, savored it, and let it out. He liked being hard. That was years ago, before Rubén found that woman who, according to Julia, turned his life around. Amadeo didn't see that much of a turnaround. His son merely went from being a poet to being a college professor and promptly forsook his language, his roots, and his family. Now he can't be bothered with his own father, except for sending the monthly stipend he and his brother pay to keep Amadeo out of their lives.

Amadeo does not know what he wants. He is waiting for night to fall, day to come. He is waiting for a presence or an absence, for a train to stop and pick him up. He is waiting for Nurse to feed him mango. Sometimes he gets tired of waiting and he remembers the morning before dawn when he was walking home from the cabaret and three men dressed in sloppy military uniforms pushed him against a wall, put a knife to his neck, and told him they were watching him. Your life is hanging by a thread, our thread, one of them said. Why had they stopped him? And why hadn't they killed him then and there? He hadn't asked these questions then, but he is asking them now. He had given money to the cause. He attended meetings and pledged to join the rebel militia in Pinar del Río. Others who had done the same had been killed on the spot, left on the street with their throats cut for the passersby to gawk at on their way to work. Julia thought it was all foolishness and did not believe him. You might as well not have come home. It is true, he insisted, but she just nodded her head as she put a plate of food on the table and went on with her housework. A man who doesn't know how to dance doesn't know how to fuck, the cabaret dancer said—no sabe singar—and he nervous at the bar hoping she would pass him by and flirt with another. He remembers her moving to the drums, he remembers her hand on his as he lit her cigarette and the sidelong look of a creature of the night. What did he know? He was twenty, falling out of love with his wife. Papi, the dancer said, take me home with you, still holding his hand well after the cigarette was lit. There was something irresistible in her voice and the way she licked her painted lips, he so full of desire he let himself say, whatever you want, mami, and ran his hand between her legs. Her sex was hot like melted butter, the pubic hair bristly and tough, and as he rubbed she kept spreading her legs wider. He remembers that. His memory is his God. As long as he has it he has his life, lived and relived as often as he wants. He remembers, he can do nothing but remember, water spraying his face, the keel cutting the waves, knife at the throat, his bed moving, someone he doesn't know pushing it out of the room, a hungry child by the side of the road, the ocean—deep indigo—bottomless grave, sirens, firemen, people running past him in the hallway. Where is Nurse? And Orderly and Garrido and Chinese Lady and Sor Diminuta? Things pass by, doors, doors, Christ crucified, nurses, patients, other beds, and he is outside the building. Everything okay, someone says, firemen inside, everything okay. Amadeo sees a cloud crossing the blue sky and he can't tell if it is a real cloud or the cloud of his memory. As a boy he played soldier on the front porch. His mother, seated, on a rocking chair, embroidered flowers on silk while singing an island air she had learned as a girl in the Canaries. The setting sun painted the walls amber and the winds of Lent brought the dust of other parts of the world. Bang, bang, I killed you, he said pointing a broomstick at an oxcart passing by. His mother kept singing the air that dropped her into a bottomless past. Bang, bang, now he shot at a passerby. Bang at a bat and bang at the sun, bang, bang, at his father riding back from the fields on his sorrel mare. Later after dinner when his father's head lolled while he sat on his wicker chair, Amadeo came behind him and pointed at his nape. It was no longer a game. Bang, bang, I killed you, he said to himself and at that moment his father's head fell to his chest, but to the boy it was not from sleep but from death. His mother in the next room sang her Canary air.

Amadeo is outside a long time. He hears the distant sound of cars whooshing by on the highway. The afternoon passes, night falls, and the crickets start singing. Parking lot lights bathe the branches above him in milky light. The wind catches them and he hears the leaves brush against each other. Dark up there above the lights, the smell is the sea where, in daytime, motorboats race back and forth. Up in the branches something is stirring. He doesn't know if it is real and of the moment or if his memory is playing tricks again and whatever is moving from branch to branch is a creature from the past inserting itself in the present— a mapache from Campeche, a jutía from Cuba, an opossum from Florida. It's bigger than that, more like a panther, and he imagines it leaping onto his bed and eating his useless toes. The hours pass and he no longer hears the whoosh of cars on pavement. Tree shadow. Blue light from the parking lot. Smell of briny sea. He can feel his breathing. He can hear his body. Finally, his bed moves out from under the tree's canopy and up above he sees clear sky with a few stars visible through the glare of the parking lot. He wishes Santa Gertrudis had burned down. He wishes he were a boy again next to his father in a fallow field across from the house. It has rained the night before and the wagons passing by earlier on the way to the cane fields have left deep furrows on the road. Amadeo is barely able to lift his legs over them. His father has given him two fat guinea hens to hold. The guinea hens dangle heavily from his hands. They flap their wings and cackle wildly as he crosses the road, taking care to lift his leg fully over the furrows. Just as he thinks he has made it safely across he relaxes his left leg and lowers his foot, which catches on the lip of the last furrow. As he falls his arms spread out in front of him and he lets go of the hens, which run off in opposite directions. He gathers himself quickly and turns to see his father on the other side of the road staring at him, then he hears his laughter and Amadeo laughs too, a deep laugh that arises from a place inside him that has no fear. He remembers days like this, when his father was just his father, and they would go to the grove back of the house and share an orange and the old man would tell him stories about life in the Canary Islands. His people were so poor, he said, that the children ate dirt to fill their stomachs and they survived on a bowl of chicken soup every night, that's all, no meat or potatoes, just soup and fried bread for months on end. Amadeo remembers their farm, its long silences, its vast sky, the unbearable heat of summer, the vegetation like a green blaze, the red earth underfoot like dried blood—sangre seca—and the moonless nights when the darkness was as thick as ink and he would float in it not sure who he was or if he was. He feels that way now. Maybe he has imagined being left behind under the tree, imagined his room as well and himself paralyzed on an imaginary bed being taken care of by imaginary beings, drooling imaginary spit, breathing imaginary air, seeing imaginary spiders, fighting an imaginary God. Maybe he has imagined his whole life from birth to the present moment. Maybe he is not real but an invention of someone else's imagination.

But if all his life is imaginary tobacco is not, not its broad green leaves growing in the slow heat then harvested and set to dry in large shadowy barns. How could he have imagined the process, the treatment of the leaf, techniques of preparation, the rolling, the cutting knife, the factory, the molds, the lector, Ibor City, an art, an industry, a life? Tobacco exists apart from Amadeo Terra and that leads to the conclusion that his life exists beyond his capacity to imagine. Amadeo remembers once hearing a lector read from a book that used a similar logic. I think about tobacco, and if tobacco is the embodiment of natural perfection, I, an imperfect being, could not have thought it up, and it must be that the idea of tobacco must have come from outside of me, from reality; therefore, tobacco exists. And if tobacco exists, then I exist because my thoughts reflect its existence. Amadeo's considerable mental efforts have exhausted him and he falls asleep. When he wakes he is back in his room. Nurse enters carrying a pan filled with warm water, several towels draped over her arm, a large brown sea sponge and a soap bar, all of which she places with great care on the rolling table. Nurse pulls the covers off in one swoop, unloosens the hospital gown, takes off his diaper and leaves him naked on the bed. He doesn't care how dirty he is. He wants her to go away so he can sleep and dream he is awake. She begins to bathe him starting with the arms and neck, then the torso, the groin and its obsolete organs, the flaccid belly, the spindly legs and feet. With the same sponge that smells as if she has used it on every patient on the floor, she washes his face and ears. She dries and dresses him, working mechanically, as if Amadeo were a piece of furniture and not a human being. Under any other circumstances her efficiency would astound him. Before leaving she covers him with a blanket. In case you get cold, she says, but Amadeo doesn't care. He does not feel cold or hot, he feels light and dark, remembers mango, the taste of deep flesh, a mass that turns and turns, whirl of beginning and end, entrance and exit, thicket of thickets, thighs without end, pulpy fruit, sea breeze on his face, tongue and more tongue, trap, triumph, tact, burrow, cave, hole, wound, cunt, tube, papaya, crack, chute, bayou, vertical smile, nether eye, lunar tide, dusk, dawn, seaquake, suckdom, rocket, stick, trunk, whistle, hose, tentacle, dong, cock, dick, tail, sausage, lance, club, prick, penetration, penetration, touch is good.

★ ★ ★

Julia once said that what attracted her to him was his face, which was, in her view, filled with optimism and devoid of doubt. Amadeo was her insurance against the war that was ravaging the country. What she didn't anticipate then was how fully she would love him later when things changed and she stopped liking him. It was a crazy war with Cubans on the side of Spain called voluntarios fighting Cubans in favor of independence calling themselves mambises. If the voluntarios who controlled Havana suspected you of being a sympathizer you were done for. If the mambises suspected you of being a loyalist, you would meet a similar fate in their hands. There were delatores, informers, everywhere, and you had to be very careful with what you did and said. When two of his friends were executed by the Spanish government, Amadeo took a machete that belonged to Julia's father and vowed to kill the first Spaniard he saw. Julia tried to stop him, but his rage was stronger than his concern. Amadeo left that afternoon at four and did not return home until dawn of the following day, drunk and disheveled and without the machete. When his father-in-law asked him what had happened, Amadeo, simmering with unspent anger, shrugged his shoulders and told the older man to go to el carajo, and he could take his daughter with him. Julia grabbed him by the arm and said we are going to find my father's machete or you can go rot in that backwater of Pinar del Río where you were born. Amadeo pulled his arm away and said he was going nowhere. Then find yourself a place to sleep because you are not doing it here in my house. Your house, he said, your house? He was not so drunk not to realize that she was right. She responded by opening the front door with such force that it banged against the wall and cracked the plaster. The old man tried to intercede, telling Julia that it was dangerous outside. That didn't stop him last night and it is not going to stop me this morning, she said. Amadeo stood uncertainly, glanced at his wife, and decided to take his chances on the street outside. He walked about half a block, never once looking back. Then he stopped, teetered like a tree about to fall, and leaned against a fence post to steady himself and think what he was going to do next: go to his friend Papo's house or return to his wife, tail between his legs. He held on to the post for some time, using all of his energy to keep from collapsing onto the sidewalk. A half-starved dog slinked by him. As the milkman passed by on his donkey, Amadeo had an uncontrollable urge to urinate. He waited for the milkman to go to the next block, then still holding on, he unbuttoned his pants and pulled out his penis. The stream jetted out in a yellow arc five feet long. He finished and wiped his hand on his pants. Then he heard footsteps approaching. He turned and saw Julia, her face smudged with tears, still very much a girl. Come home, she said with her hands on her hips. We will look for the machete later. It cannot be found, he said. Why not? Because it is not lost. I sold it. You sold it? To buy rum at a bodega. Who did you sell it to? A man who wanted to kill Spaniards more than I did. That machete was worthless, he added. I will buy your father a better one. He came close to her and they walked home together, she holding him to keep him from falling, he trying to stand straight so that the neighbors would not think that Julia had a drunk for a husband.

It has been quiet for several days, but suddenly the woman across the hall is screaming again. He has never seen her but imagines her pale and toothless with white hair splaying in all directions. She smells like the old do, like he does, of urine and the crust of decay, of dried-out flesh and worn-out skin. Her legs have been amputated and cataracts blear her vision. Her vocabulary has been reduced to ten words. Someone named Mari has placed her here, after being driven crazy by the old lady at home and driving her husband crazy and her children and all the aides that came and went crazy over the years because they couldn't deal with Mari, Mariii, come here, repeated constantly, brainlessly, from the moment of waking to the moment of sleep. What anguish Mari must have gone through to contradict her vow that she would never abandon her mother in a nursing home! She would take care of her at home, she would have her own room, she would die surrounded by family. Mari, Mariii, come here and Mari is nowhere to be found because early on she was so ashamed, so pained by her visits that she stopped coming altogether. Eventually, just to make her life a little easier, she found other things and people to occupy her. A few times a month thoughts of her mother creep into her mind and prick her conscience. Her eyes spring a few tears, she blows her nose and goes on with her day. Mari, Mariii, come here. Forget it, Lady, Mari is at work or attending her granddaughter's piano concert or fixing dinner for her husband. Mari is not coming, and she will not come until she receives a phone call telling her we are very sorry, Mrs. Mengana, your mother passed away early this morning. We would like you to come immediately to make the necessary arrangements. Mari will be guilt-ridden, devastated. Her husband and children will console her. Abuela couldn't live forever, she died peacefully, in the hands of God, etc. They will not notice (her tears are so copious, her face so twisted by grief) that underneath it all, Mari is relieved. She can now take a deep breath and live her life without the burden of her mother. Because, you see, although she is far away, she can hear you calling, she can hear that screechy voice of yours like a hoarse jackass, Mari, Mariii, as clearly as I can hear it, and once you die, she will no longer have to listen to it. Just as I long for you to die, Mrs. Fulana, so does your daughter. One day, if I happen to be unlucky enough to outlast you, I will no longer hear your voice and then I will know you are gone, and it will be quiet here again, and I can think of how my sons have turned their backs on me.

People are always leaving Santa Gertrudis and Amadeo knows perfectly well what that means. First, there was Chinese Lady. Then out went Arialdo, who hated women. He would ride the wheelchair into Amadeo's room and tell him all the despicable things his mother used to do to him when he was a child. He rolled up his sleeves and showed Amadeo the multiple scars on his arms, the consequences of his mother's peculiar love. Round face, sharply pointed eyebrows, bulging sleepy eyes. Frying onions made him swoon, perfume made him choke. He disappeared the first year of Amadeo's stay, when he still believed that patients left Santa Gertrudis because they got better. There was Apollonia, who walked around with a constant headache and whose face was always broken out in hives—she was allergic to life—and Garrido whom he has not seen in some time, and others, nameless mostly, who passed by his room or whom he saw in the common hall when Nurse still took him there. Just before he falls asleep he remembers a vast expanse of sugar cane, he remembers the still air, the sun beating down on the red earth and far off in the distance a ceiba tree that was haunted by the spirits of murdered slaves. Summer stillness, summer heat, time at a standstill, a loud buzzing in his ear. He remembers turning around, he remembers a hummingbird hovering inches from his nose.

madeo overhears Nurse in the hallway singing along with the radio. Her voice, flat, off-key, enters him like a tiny worm of emotion and awakens in him a vestige of physical desire. Music he never thought of as an end in itself but as a way of seducing a woman, an enticement to buy lottery tickets, or as background to elephants dancing in the circus. Now music is a crux. He feels an overwhelming sense of longing for his childhood; it doesn't matter how unhappy it might seem in retrospect because then it was neither happy nor unhappy. It was childhood: the pain of his father's lashings, the dogs having sex behind the larder, the toads jumping on his thighs at night as he crossed the backyard, the day he stood on his toes on a water barrel to see the circus women dancing to trumpets and drums. He remembers the dark bellies beaded with sweat, the blur of hips, the laughter, the hands twirling in the air like butterflies. The song went, Lamartina López se tragó una lagartija, en la noche se dormía y en el día se entendía con un mozo de los buenos y una vieja matutina. Once a year the circus came to San Juan y Martínez. It traveled in its own train bringing hundreds of crates and caged animals from every part of the world. The train stopped at the cattle depot and unloaded its cargo, after which the circus troupe paraded down the main street to the other side of town where it set up its tents in a field that once belonged to Arturo Longo, the town butcher, a man of legendary appetites and evil reputation. Amadeo watched from the corner of Martí and Palma Streets as the performers passed by, dressed in exotic costumes from Africa and the Cochin-China, eating fire, performing magic tricks, and tumbling from sidewalk to sidewalk. He remembers a girl his age with white patent leather sandals, her body moving with the confidence of an adult, her lips painted red, her eyelids painted blue. Amadeo could feel his heart in his throat, his hands trembling, sweat building in the small of his back. A marching band came by, the musicians dressed in military uniforms discarded from a European war, followed by carts bearing an emaciated tiger, a mangy bear, and two declawed lions in their cages, which were opened at different points during the traverse so that the trainer could enter and put his head inside the mouth of one of the beasts. At the rear were two elephants driven by a man people called the fakir because he wore a turban and a silk cape. He prodded the pachyderms with a long stick and yelled at them in a language Amadeo could not understand and that filled him with wonder about the ancient mysteries of the Orient. But it was the women dancing with the girl at their center that he thought about in the sleepless nights following the circus's arrival. He saved all he could during the year in order to buy a ticket and when he didn't have enough, he stole the rest from a tin can his mother kept under the bed. His last year in San Juan y Martínez the circus came as usual in late October but the girl wasn't there. In her place a small dog dressed like a clown did foolish tricks. Amadeo's head rattled with the broken glass of disappointment and in his mouth lingered the raw metal taste of shame.

He remembers overhearing the men at the corner talking of the woman who had sex with a donkey and the ex-slave who could break a stack of twelve lard crackers with his foot-long penis. And you, boy, what do you want?

It was the carpenter who built his father's weasel traps. Amadeo looked down at the ground and said nothing. Mind your business and go back to your toys, the man said and continued describing how the hawker announced el Negro Tulún and his African penis and the black man appeared dressed in a white robe. The hawker stacked the crackers carefully on a stool and el Negro Tulún disrobed exposing his black hose, which he swung in an arc and shattered the crackers from top to bottom. I've never seen anything like it, said the carpenter. Amadeo's mind was filled with thoughts of the gypsy girl which blended with images of el Negro Tulún and the donkey woman. It is always the same with guajiros, country people, Amadeo thinks, drawn to the lowest examples of human behavior. Country people, his father used to say, then sell them anything they would buy—straw hats, leather boots, slab bacon and yuca, brooms, buckets, cough syrup made from kerosene. He wrote everything in his little book and waited for payday when the guajiros stood in line to pay their bills and buy firewater and rum with the leftover money. Amadeo's father grew rich from the guajiros, but he threw his wealth away on endless sessions of necromancy run by a blind woman who had learned her black art in the capital. Boy, move away or I'll smack you a good one. Amadeo didn't move. He was waiting for the circus to pass, hoping to see something that would erase his longing and confusion, when the carpenter's big meaty hand came in his direction. Amadeo arched his head back and the carpenter's hand swung past. The carpenter lost his balance and almost fell, then he came back swinging awkwardly with the other hand closed in a fist, this time catching Amadeo on the temple with such force that the blow lifted the boy off the ground and threw him against a wall. When Amadeo came to, the parade had gone by and the crowd at the corner had dispersed. Through the buzzing in his right ear he could hear the far-off sound of the circus tents going up.

Today Amadeo awaits, none too happily, a visit from the physical therapist. His name is Joaquín and he usually comes dressed in a white uniform, although about a year ago he entered Amadeo's room in his street clothes. Earlier that morning one of the patients had thrown up all over his uniform and he had to change back into his tie, jacket, two-toned shoes in which that same night he would go visit his girlfriend. This is the country of vomit and shit, he said to Amadeo as he rubbed his feet. If anybody dirties me up again, I am quitting. Time has not been generous to Joaquín. He is bald, and his once athletic body (he was a shot-putter in high school) has fallen into decadence. He

has that belly that men develop after forty and that nothing, outside of extreme dietetic practices, will diminish.
His round Galician grocer's face is inhabited by the resignation of the bachelor (the girlfriend didn't work out).
Joaquín comes every two weeks, performs exercises on
Amadeo's legs and arms (raise and bend, raise and bend)
and maintains an incessant monologue in which he plumbs
the depths of banality while he works on Amadeo's body.
Today, for example, he begins with a highly detailed de-
scription of the varicose veins that have developed in his
left testicle and are causing him great discomfort. The
doctor has assured him that he should not worry, they are
benign, but the discomfort persists as does the worry that
they presage something much more serious. This is the
word he uses: presage. Joaquín is prone to using words that
are out of the range of most people's vocabulary but he
hasn't stumped Amadeo yet. Pretentious to the extreme,
it is apparent that Joaquín, being a good bachelor, has no
worry but himself. He has a cat named Perico at home, a
small unobtrusive pet that fills the void in his life. Amadeo
knows more about Perico than he cares—his eating habits, his fear of darkness, the long tail that shakes sideways
when he is happy, how he hides under the bed when it
thunders and stretches along the windowsill to catch the
sun, how he likes to sleep curled next to Joaquín. Better a

cat than a floppy mastodontic wife, the type who takes up most of the space her husband would otherwise inhabit. This thought brings to mind Amadeo's Aunt Concha, greasy and monumental, who spent her afternoons seated in a divan in her house breathing, no, masticating the thick tropical air, complaining constantly about the suffocating heat and cursing the maids whom she kept anxiously fluttering around her. The maids were there to satisfy her wishes: cold water, hot coffee, and the huge pots of food— Madrid tripe, creole stew, Asturian bean soup—that Concha consumed every afternoon. The younger members of the family, for whom corpulence alone did not inspire the respect it did in the old days, called her the walrus behind her back, because in addition to her carnal volume, Aunt Concha had a rather thick mustache and a large mole on her chin from which grew three long hairs. She was married to a man named Filiberto, a clerk at the neighborhood hardware store who lived in the shadows of her corpulence. When he came home late from work, which he did several times a week (he was, by all accounts, a conscientious and dedicated worker), Aunt Concha turned into a great bellows of ire. The pale skin of her cheeks became red and her eyes that once were green, perhaps even beautiful, came out of their sockets swollen, covered with a yellow film. When she could no longer contain herself, she would scream, I smell something! That Filiberto is cheating on me! Of course no one in the family could imagine Filiberto with another woman. He was very thin with an oversized head the shape of a güiro gourd, and his lack of personality inspired much more pity than disdain. The man was forever tormented by Aunt Concha's insults and sailor's language and nobody faulted him for arriving home late once in a while, after all business is business, and if the boss says you have to stay late, you stay late. On those nights Filiberto got home after nine, he found his wife boiling on the divan, her great walrus body marooned in the vapors of the living room, exhaling an acrid stench. He listened to her a moment, said his good nights, and kept going to the bedroom where he locked himself up until the following morning. Many years after both their deaths, the family learned that Aunt Concha had been right: Filiberto had been unfaithful to her with a beautiful woman fifteen years his junior who loved him a great deal and gave him everything that Aunt Concha couldn't provide: peace, pleasure, and four endearing children.

The therapy session ends after fifteen minutes and Joaquín sits down to dry his bald pate. He is speaking about his apartment, about the weather, about a woman named Maruca in room 503, poor thing, she is spewing blood through her seven orifices. Amadeo thinks there are nine, not seven. He blinks to see if Joaquín corrects himself, but no, he has gone on to another topic that Amadeo cannot quite follow, and now he is talking about his new Ford which has broken down three times in one month, those cars are not good, Buicks on the other hand are the best, but they are expensive, with my salary I could never afford one. Amadeo wants to interrupt and talk about the last car he owned, a green '37 Buick that was a gorgeous machine and turned everyone's head as he drove down La Séptima, but even if he could he doubts Joaquín would listen. The truth is life has gotten so expensive I am thinking of getting a job on weekends to make ends meet, especially now that I have decided to remodel the apartment. My friend Alberto the Butcher promised to help me and, you may ask, what does a butcher know about remodeling, but the truth is the boy knows about everything, I mean, I get these awful headaches that used to lay me out flat in the old days, and he gave me the remedy, a plaster of mustard and firewater he learned from his grandmother that I place on the side of the head where the pain is and in half an hour it is gone, I inherited the headaches from my mother, sometimes she would spend a whole week in bed retching from the pain, poor woman, had she only known about the plaster. After they made Alberto the Butcher they broke the mold. He is simply unique.

Sometimes he brings me a whole tenderloin as a gift and he cuts it up into steak, beef cubes, a chunk for grinding into picadillo, and a spectacular roast which is a true delight. He does it all in my kitchen, clearing the counter—I am not the neatest housekeeper—and getting right to work with his knife. In half an hour Alberto is done, but he doesn't stop there, besides a butcher he is a chef d'haute cuisine, and if he is in the mood, he will prepare a pot roast worthy of the most discriminating kitchens in Europe. He makes it look easy, too. He throws onion, green pepper, garlic, laurel, sour orange—which he goes through great effort to get, but it is much better than plain lemon, isn't it?—cooking wine, and I don't know what else into the pot; then he adds the meat and cooks it in slow heat. I tell you the man is an alchemist, what comes out of the pot is edible gold. I am taking down a wall that divides the kitchen from the living room to enhance the space. Divisions are anti-aesthetic, aren't they? Besides, Alberto is making me some shelving for my Lladró collection. I mean, I have two hundred figures stored and what's the use of having a collection if you can't display it?

Joaquín might have had a girlfriend in the remote past, but at this point in his life he talks and behaves like a man whose pants are on backwards. Not that it matters much. Amadeo feels nothing that isn't thought, which is the same as saying essence, coursing through his veins. His life has been reduced to that. It is as if God had played a final practical joke before abandoning him. I am going to take away your body so that you will know what it is like to be pure spirit. And pure solitude, Amadeo adds. I have been told that you don't need to ask permission of the board in order to tear down an internal wall, Joaquín says. Speak to me about what you feel at night when you are all alone, Amadeo implores him. But Joaquín is not interested in these things. He prefers to focus on the window treatment he has chosen for the living room windows—a baroque brown and beige pattern he saw in a fashion magazine— and the color of the walls—yellow, with beige trim around the casements. That which he speaks of with such passion— his daily life—is Joaquín's satisfaction, just as tobacco, which remains in his memory as the source of his passion, used to be for Amadeo. Amadeo concludes that Joaquín is the fortunate one, finding interest in the minutiae of daily life. Joaquín rises from his chair and Amadeo wants to tell him to stay longer, keep talking about his window treatments, the bedspread he bought last week, the exquisite meals he and Alberto share. What is the worth of tobacco? Amadeo blinks several times, as if this meant anything to Joaquín, who pats his forehead a few more times, says, Ay princesa, ¡qué calor! and leaves.

★　★　★

It is the day of San Juan and a man is hanging from a tree. His face is tinged red from a bonfire a few feet away. To the right of Amadeo someone is cheering; to his left a roller he knows but whose name he cannot remember is lighting a cigar, carefully singeing the tip with the flame before taking the first puff. A third man he has never seen before pokes the hanged man with a stick and makes him twirl, then hits him across the back as if he were trying to break a piñata. Cabrón italiano, Amadeo hears. Scab bastard. And the phrases are coming out of his own mouth, a vacuous anger building in his chest. He wants to kill every strikebreaker in Tampa, hang them from every tree so they know who owns this town. Have no pity on the enemy. That is what he tells Julia that night when he gets home while she rages at him for letting it happen, for not having the courage to save an innocent man. You killed him, you coward, she says. Only his wife can speak to him that way. I did not, he answers with too much defensiveness in his voice. You're as guilty as the man who whipped the horse. The man's face, he thinks, was blue wax, tongue between his lips and a ridge of skin the rope raised under the jaw. They say men get an erection when they are hanged but Amadeo refused to look down there. Pobre diablo, he probably didn't know what a scab was. Amadeo cannot erase the hanged man from his memory. The face becomes his son's. He cannot erase all the darkness around him and Julia walking into the kitchen and his boys beyond the darkness where he cannot reach them.

Suddenly Amadeo is lifted out of the bed and into his chair. Mr. Terra, he hears Nurse's dim voice. Mr. Terra, it is a beautiful day outside. Orderly, too, says something but it is unintelligible. Amadeo sees the sunlight on the water and he wants to be alone. He wants the company of the dead. It is the living who refuse to enter the world of darkness. They are leaving, Nurse and Orderly are leaving and he is seated by the window where he can observe the clouds, gray and white, thousands of clouds passing over the water that wants to be blue but is never quite that color. The sea is a song that repeats itself. The clouds tilt their heads to listen. Amadeo remembers a boy from their neighborhood who sang day and night to erase, he said, the sadness of the world. One day he left to seek his fortune and never returned. People leave, death comes near. That was long ago when Amadeo was a young man and he was beginning to learn the limits of his happiness. After two years of marriage, he took any opportunity to leave the house and get away from Julia and her incessant talk about the curtains, the settee, the leak on the kitchen roof, the grocer's bill, the room they were planning to add to accommodate the child coming in six months, the blocked well pipe, the mousetraps under the floor boards, the featherbed she had ordered, the rocking chair she bought on credit, money worries, morning sickness, and all the other things that occupy a woman within the confines of her household. He would walk to the end of the block after dinner and light his cigar. Sometimes he met a neighbor and they would have a chat. That's how he met the boy and heard his songs about the fragrance of gardenias and the pains of love. Other times he watched the volantas clop by driven by well-dressed gentlemen and their carefree ladies. He observed the confident manner in which the men clutched the reins and urged the horse to go faster while the women held their hats and laughed. His wife was home pregnant and the world was rushing by. Once, after the sun went down, he walked past the corner two blocks to where the street curved and headed downhill. The smell of war lingered in the air but the night was peaceful, all the houses dark except for one at the corner where a light was flickering. He heard singing and, getting closer, he realized it was the boy's voice coming from inside. He sat down on the wooden sidewalk and listened. It was a song about lovers walking on the beach and the waves washing over their feet. For a moment the tune entered him and rushed through his veins. The hair at the back of his neck bristled and his ears burned. Then the music stopped. He stood and looked down at his shoes, dusty and cracked, and realized he was as exposed as a man can be in the city on a moonless night. At home he couldn't stand the boredom, the possibility of the present repeated into a future without end. Up above the sky was filled with stars. Around him the city lay silent. Some force he could sense but could not name kept him from falling through the ground and disappearing into the earth. It was like being inside someone else's dream and he became afraid he would never leave it. Amadeo knocked several times on the door. He wanted to talk with the boy, make sure the singing had not been an invention of his needy brain. No one answered and he never heard the tune again. Instead there is Nurse and her screechy voice, the radio in the hall from which come muted ballads and tinny dance tunes. Julia never sang or hummed but sometimes she whistled and sometimes, when she didn't think anyone was looking, she danced by herself in the kitchen or out in the garden. Amadeo remembers her swaying hips before the tomato plants and he wants to laugh, but the lips won't spread, the laugh won't come. He drools instead and this time Nurse, who is in the room cleaning up, rushes to the side of the bed and slaps him across the face. Amadeo is stunned. His eyes want to pop out of their sockets; they fill with tears. He is looking through a red tunnel at her; he burns white hot. Truth is, the slap has had its desired effect and he has stopped drooling. Nurse looms over him saying nothing, but in her posture and demeanor are all the words she will ever need for this moment: Mr. Terra, sir, you have led me to this. I have cleaned you time and again, Mr. Terra, you have no one to blame but yourself. She turns away and leaves the room. Amadeo hears the swish-swoosh of her massive thighs rubbing against each other as she re- treats until the sound disappears and there is only the beating of his heart and the memory of the memory of the song about lovers on the beach or later, much later, mixed in somehow with that, the music of cheap bars he frequented where women danced for him stripping off their clothes one piece at a time, their bodies glistening with sweat, their laughter drowning out the music and he throwing money at them until he had nothing left but an empty space in his chest where the winds of his be- trayal blew. Where is the girl now who danced to the drums? Where is the boy singing in the night? He went out in search of a richer life but he came home with smoke in his hands, the smell of women on his body, the taste of liquor in his mouth. Nurse wiping the rolling table,

Nurse slapping him, Nurse apologetic. She reappears with Orderly who is carrying a plastic tube attached to an enema bottle. Nurse spreads Amadeo's legs while Orderly inserts the tube. They are enjoying this. Amadeo can see it in their faces. The solution is poured into him and he feels a rumbling inside like a temblor in his entrails, then all of him coming out as if a dam had burst. What he loses: fecal water pouring into the basin. What he gains: space for more.

Amadeo is a wild dog roaming the night. When he isn't searching for a domino game he is searching for a cockfight, when he isn't searching for a cockfight, he is looking for a woman. Amadeo wants to find whatever makes him feel alive, away from the domestic Sargasso that threatens to drown him. On one of those nights when a cold wet wind is blowing from the north and there are no cockfights or women anywhere, he sees a girl sitting in the Parque Central with her parents. They, too, have been driven to the city by the endless warring and Amadeo takes pity on their ragged clothes and the startled forlorn eyes of people not used to the city. He walks on to the other end of the park then circles back to where the family is sitting, introduces himself, and says he knows a place where they can stay the night, which is not true. He leads them out of the park into the city down Calle

Reina thinking he will have to take them home to Julia and she will become angry again, how dare he bring country strangers to stay at their house! Then he remembers a roller at the cigar factory whose mother runs a boarding house twenty blocks from the park close to Vedado and he takes them there, hoping there are rooms available. The girl, Ana, is fourteen, dark haired with big blue eyes that give off a wild, piercing energy. As they walk her bony arms begin to shiver from the cold. Amadeo has a sudden urge to bring her close to him. Her shoulders seem so frail they would crumble from the weight of his arm. They are in luck. His friend's mother has two rooms on the first floor behind the kitchen. Amadeo pays for a week in advance against the protests of the father, who wants no charity. Would you rather have your daughter catch her death in the cold, Amadeo asks him in a friendly enough manner. His eyes, sharp and filled with authority, are fixed on the older man who has no option but to shake his head and turn away.

Amadeo's vision glazes over and he loses focus of the things in front of him—the pictures of the clown and the mountains, the pine veneer dresser. This happens to him sometimes when he is remembering. Only the past is clearly before him. If he hears anything—Nurse singing under her breath, for example—it becomes a part of what he is remembering. And so he hears Ana singing in Nurse's falsetto the same songs Nurse knows. He visits the rooming house once a week at first, to make sure Ana and her parents are all right. The father is selling candy on the streets; the mother irons for the landlady. It is okay, Amadeo thinks, that he is fond of her. Ana is like a younger sister to him. They sit on the edge of the bed while she sings and Amadeo talks about tobacco, his colleagues at the factory, the endless war that no one wants but no one knows how to end. Ana sits with her hands folded on her lap or else plays with a wooden abacus he has brought her. After an hour or two he gets up, kisses her on the cheek, and gives her mother, who is ironing in the front room, some money on the way out. One day Ana puts her abacus down, says she is tired, and lies back on the bed. Amadeo leans over and kisses her, first on the cheek, then he slides his lips over hers. Ana giggles and tries to squirm free but his weight is too much for her. He remembers her fresh young smell and the alabaster skin of her neck punctuated by a few dark moles. He remembers her soft belly and hard breasts, him entering her, Ana whimpering, Ana smiling; he remembers feeling shame afterwards and giving the mother twice the usual amount and walking into the sun-washed alley leading to the street, avoiding Julia that night, vowing to himself not to return to the rooming house but returning anyway. His visits to Ana go on much the same way for several months. Sometimes he brings food for the family, sometimes a dress for the girl he buys cheaply on the street. At home Julia complains that there isn't enough money to pay bills. She has been using the money they were saving for the baby's layette to pay the grocer, and the milkman is threatening to stop delivery. Using a system of logic he can no longer remember, he convinces himself that Julia is not suspicious, that her worries have no deeper root. One afternoon while he is frolicking in bed with Ana there is a loud commotion in the other room. Amadeo wraps a bedsheet around himself, opens the door and finds Julia with her huge belly pointing a revolver at Ana's mother's head. The mother, who is as frail as a reed and pale as the sheet Amadeo is wearing, stands silently in place. Her toothless mouth is agape and her hands are shaking at her sides. Take your guajira whore of a daughter and get out of the city, Julia says. We will, we will, the mother says, although it comes out sounding like weeo, weeo. Julia then pivots slowly and points the gun at Amadeo. Inexplicably, neither fear nor remorse enters his mind but a desire to know how she has found the rooming house and where she has gotten the gun, a huge revolver she holds up with both hands. He is certain that Julia will not shoot him and just as he is about to break into a smile, the gun goes off and a bullet whizzes past his head. She looks at him without saying anything, then lowers the weapon and leaves. Amadeo is left standing in the doorway infected by a paralysis of the will, not knowing whether to laugh or run after his wife. Behind him, Ana, naked and angelic and indifferent, lies in bed picking her navel. Then the mother, gathering all the strength of her wisp of a body, throws herself at him with such fierceness that he falls to the floor. She tries to kick him and misses, tries again and catches him on the thigh. He can hear Ana giggling on the bed and all he can do is pick up his clothes and rush out, sneaking out the back of the rooming house so the landlady won't see him.

Amadeo's eyesight gains focus and he thinks very hard trying to remember how old he was then. He was living in Tampa. No. The war was still going on. He was in Havana. He was twenty-two, twenty-one, Julia pregnant with Rubén or was Rubén already born and she was pregnant with Pastor? He thought he was falling out of love with Julia, but he was just bored with routine. Was that his fault? It is Julia he wants next to him now. He thinks of her as a young woman when the wildness still ran in her and a mere touch of his hand was enough to set her on fire. Dishes were left undone, laundry unwashed, pots on the stove until the burning smell entered the bedroom and woke them from their ardor. If they found the food scorched, they forgot about eating and went back to the feast of their bodies the rest of the night. At dawn they heard the roosters crowing across the city and they laughed.

Of late Amadeo has been dreaming that he is an aristocrat. He sits on a thronelike chair and doesn't need to speak because all his needs and wants are immediately known and satisfied by a coterie of servants who surround him. There is one in charge of seafood, another whose specialty is beef, a third who provides the most exquisite liquors. If he wants oysters, a plate of them appears magically before him. If lobster strikes his fancy, along come a pair with huge claws cracked and dressed, surrounded by bowlfuls of drawn butter, aioli, and enchilado sauce on a silver plate; beer, barrels of it, and the best Bordeaux and grand cru champagne. In one version of the dream he has the urge to read and the servants carry him in a palanquin to a library. There, a blind librarian who has read every book ever written is sitting at a table waiting for him. After learning what kind of book Amadeo wishes to read, the librarian walks to the stacks and returns with several Amadeo recognizes—*Candide, The Idiot,* the essays of Montaigne. Amadeo takes them and begins reading in his bedroom but is distracted by a fantasy in which he is having sex with two young women. Most of the time the dream stops here with the full enjoyment of the abundance that is a measure of his power. Sometimes, however, an old woman appears who sits on a smaller chair next to his and complains about his behavior. The woman's face is bleared most of the time. In one version she is Julia; in another she is his mother, and, on one occasion, she is both. The dream, which he has had with increasing frequency the last few months, portends no good: a life lived between motherly grief and wifely recrimination. In his life he never worried about these things but went about the unencumbered pursuit of pleasure. He impresses himself with this last phrase, which he can poorly translate into Spanish as la libre búsqueda del placer, or more simply put in Cuban as la jodedera. He worked as much as he had to, like a beast of burden sometimes, but he never thought twice about satisfying his urges when they needed satisfying. Now he dreams about the angel of doubt and the angel of denial and it is when the dream gets to this point that he awakes, breathing heavily and wishing that it were daytime and he would not have to sleep anymore. The dream comes in shards that he pieces together once he is awake. The key has to do with the old woman. If she were not part of the dream he would only take it as some sort of manifestation of unsatisfied desire. In other words, it would be a dream of frustration. The appearance of the two people in his life who tried to curtail his appetites just as the young girls are squirming all over him complicate the dream and make it a source of endless rumination.

Whether he wakes out of a dream or deep sleep, Amadeo's eyes are wide open before dawn most mornings and then he waits, first for the song of birds in the trees below, which he can hear when the air conditioning is not running, followed by the lazy light of dawn, which joins with the light from the driveway below and in time overwhelms it. There are the stirrings of the nurses outside and faint conversation between them about domestic matters, dinner the night before or the dress one of them bought for her daughter at the Sears & Roebuck or the latest installment in their favorite soap opera—a story about infidelity and betrayal. The lady across the hall will start calling for Mari and Garrido might come asking for his shoelaces and the world will repeat itself once again as it has done day after day, month after month ever since Amadeo has known it.

Nurse comes today accompanied by Doctor who has not paid a visit in several weeks. He is unshaven and his

eyes are puffy from lack of sleep. On his face is the damp
pallor of one who has drunk too much the night before.
When Doctor leans over him, Amadeo is overcome by his
breath, which smells like a blend of formaldehyde and
curdled milk. Behind him is Nurse, blond and enormous,
blocking the light from the window. Doctor continues the
checkup, poking here, poking there, shining a light into
Amadeo's eyes, taking off Amadeo's diaper—it is soiled,
Nurse, let's get a stool sample—putting on a rubber glove
and checking around inside, finally declaring in a voice
with a homey affectation, You're healthy as a young colt,
Mr. Terra. The combination of Doctor's breath and his
own feces is making Amadeo nauseated. He can feel his
stomach churning upward and sideways and a burning
headache spreading across his forehead like lava. As Doctor
bends over one last time to use his stethoscope Amadeo's
peristalsis goes into full reversal and splashes on Doctor's
face. Doctor straightens up horrified. Nurse, who has been
passive and silent next to Doctor during the examination,
shifts immediately into action, wiping Doctor's face and
stethoscope with one of the small hand towels that abound
in Santa Gertrudis. Looking helpless, Doctor sits down on
the chair next to the bed, takes off his glasses and covers
his face with his free hand. It has obviously not been a good
day for him, or a good life for that matter, but Amadeo

does not have the luxury of feeling sorry for him. When Nurse finishes wiping Doctor, she says nothing, nothing at all as she leads him away. She returns to change Amadeo and leaves immediately. And indeed Amadeo's punishment seems to be that he is ignored the rest of the morning. It is not until lunchtime, when he is swooning with hunger, that someone enters the room. It is Sor Diminuta, bringing with her a tray of baby food and two of the small white towels draped over her arm. Amadeo is beside himself. If only he could get up and greet her in the proper manner, take her by the arm, ask her how she's been. He goes through all these things in his mind, has full conversations with her, prepares tea (he puts a little rum in his) and brings out cookies. They talk about the convent, her fellow nuns, about God and the angels, about the heat and humidity of Florida. Amadeo makes a comment about her heavy garment, how rough and uncomfortable it must feel on her skin, how it must make her sweat (perhaps he can insinuate the need for daily bathing in such a climate). Sor Diminuta ignores the comment and instead she asks him about his life as a cigar worker. You cannot have a better life, he says. You work to give others pleasure. Tobacco is the purest product in the world. There were days I'd roll one hundred, two hundred. To make cigars you must have delicacy and strength in your hands, you must possess a clear mind and you must be passionate to make the best cigar. You must be around tobacco many years and practice until whatever comes from your hands is perfect. You give it up, you let the smoker smoke. Even as Amadeo is speaking he realizes that what he is saying must be boring and that he is merely trying to impress Sor Diminuta. If he'd been a glass blower, he'd be waxing poetic about silica. Sor Diminuta is cleaning his body. He stops and thinks and tries to remember what it is like to have a woman's hands touching him but only Nurse comes to mind with her stumpy fingers and coarse manners. Sor Diminuta is different. She is so small that her hands are like feathery birds running up and down his thighs, moving his testicles and penis out of the way, wiping his anus as one wipes a well-calibrated instrument. He is getting hard now. Sor Diminuta is floating over him in her brown habit, Sor Diminuta is taking him in her mouth, she is sitting on him, rocking back and forth. Sor Diminuta smells like cumin and hay (or was that Julia?), Sor Diminuta is hot, she is looking up to heaven, she is crying out Jesus Christ Almighty, singing, hitting the high notes, the low. She is an angel, a fallen one. She is done cleaning and dressing him and stands over him smiling in her holy nunlike fashion. If she only knew what she has done in his mind. Sabrosona! He blinks yes several times to see if she understands, but blinking is his own impenetrable language and all she does is smile some more and rub his forehead.

Amadeo doesn't know if he is awake or asleep, if he is dreaming or fantasizing or dreaming his fantasy. In his next dream he sits on a throne holding a huge basket of rotting fruit on his lap which fills the air around him with flies. He wants one of the servants to take the fruit away but they are otherwise occupied and no matter how hard he tries to get their attention they walk by him as if he didn't exist. Without a voice he cannot command them; without strength in his arms he is unable to lift the basket, which soon, on its own, slides off his lap. The servants ignore him still but he is glad to be rid of the weight that was pinning him down. In the next part of the dream he sees that his groin is crawling with rabbits. They are coming out of his britches, jumping onto the floor and hopping in every direction. Then Julia appears in front of him as a very old woman carrying Albertico. His arm is hanging down and his head is leaning against Julia's chest. Amadeo is desperate to see the boy's face, but when Albertico turns it toward him, it is covered with large black spiders. A door closes and Amadeo wakes up. Whenever he remembers this dream he feels like he is sweating from the inside. Now more than ever, he would like to stand and walk away into sun so hot, ice so cold he will lose the memory of that day. Out the window the sky is hazy white and far off over the ocean a dark cloud is threatening rain. The water is choppy and gray. Something is about to break open, and to allay his anxiety he starts to count blinks. He reaches thirty, then goes to fifty and continues to one hundred. Beyond that each blink gets increasingly difficult, and he wants to stop but he fights the urge and continues counting. At two hundred his eyelids weigh on his eyeballs as if they were made of lead. The instinct is to keep them closed but he forces them open each time, using all his concentration to keep from losing count. By three hundred fifty his eyeballs are dry, the lids scraping against them like sandpaper. He counts past five hundred, an excruciating number. At seven hundred he reaches a wide, level expanse where effort becomes ease and by one thousand it doesn't feel like counting at all. Later, at around fourteen or fifteen hundred, he hears a noise like a large door closing every time the lids swivel over the ball of his eyes. Light, dark, light, dark, each number defining one or the other in the narrow straight line of arithmetic, after which blinking finally stops and the eye is an orb in a numberless universe. He knows he is not there yet. All that progression, all that movement forward to seventeen hundred and beyond where blinking loses purpose and sight is the same as non-sight. He stops and focuses on Sor Diminuta who is looking at him with great concern. Mr. Terra, she says. Mr. Terra, he hears her calling from a great distance. Amadeo tries to reassure her by blinking but his eyes are fixed on the open position and no effort on his part will force them closed. He wants to make love to her again, he wants to lift her habit and open her coffers, smell that loba smell of hers. He wants this not to be a dream. Julia intrudes, carrying Albertico, and the rabbits leaping out of his groin.

In Tampa, when Albertico was seven, he and Julia played a game in which he gave her a word and she would have to find another word within it. In perro she found pero; in lengua she found auge; in nariz she found raíz. It was a good game and Albertico used to get so worked up sometimes he would wet his pants: arroz, zorra; frijol, fijo; caballo, bala; traje, teja; árbol, labor. No matter what word Albertico thought up, Julia would find the one hidden inside. Amadeo tried reversing roles once and Albertico stumped him with the first word he gave him: bobo. There is always a word hidden inside another, Julia said, and you will always find the sound of it inside yourself. She never told him what the hidden word was inside bobo, and he has just discovered it: bobo. The hidden word is the word itself.

Sor Diminuta is leaning over him, her face so close to his he can smell her breath—tea with cardamom. She has a long, delicate neck, she has corrugated nipples, she has freckles on her chest, she has a mole in the middle of her back he can feel when she straddles him. But that's Julia's mole. Her mother had it and her grandfather before that, a family mark. It feels like a bloated tick, he said. Don't touch it, she said. Hard not to when you're sitting on top of me. We won't do that anymore, she said. But you like it, he said. Sometimes, she said, raising herself up by her arms and grinding herself into him in a circular motion until she screamed.

I'm counting blinks, Sor Diminuta. Why? It keep things moving, keeps the mind floating. I've spent my whole life counting. You must be good at it, she says. As good as you are at praying. Sor Diminuta takes a damp towel and pats his forehead. Wild dog, that's what my wife called me. Perro salvaje. He looks up at her sideways: the face is not the nun's but his mother's and he is burning with fever. Behind her, illumined by candlelight, is someone he does not recognize. She is dressed in black and is holding a prayer book and has been in the room ever since he got the fever. A doctor comes and shakes his head. His father at the door, other people bustling in and out. A priest anoints him, speaking in Latin. Next thing he knows it is morning and the lady who held the prayer book is opening the windows, letting in the fresh warm air and the sounds of the barnyard. Sor Diminuta says she is leaving. Wild dog, he does not want her to leave, he wags his tail. Stay, stay, he stands on his rear legs pawing her arms. He drops down on all fours and runs twice around her barking. Wild dog, wild dog, soul coming out of him, a blur of brown habit flying out the door.

On his days off Amadeo spends hours looking at Julia's garden. To the right of the yard against the fence she has planted morning glories that twirl about the poles in great profusion. In the morning the purple and white blossoms open to the sun and draw humming-birds by the dozen. Along the other fence there are red and white roses the size of a man's fist and closer to the house is a gardenia bush that perfumes the air at dusk. Squarely in the middle, to the left of the path that leads to the outhouse, Julia has her vegetable plot. Depending on the year, she plants tomatoes, squash, corn, large green peppers, radishes the size of lemons, and always, without fail, calabazas and yuca. There are insects buzzing around her in the morning sunlight—bumblebees and white and yellow butterflies—and the occasional garter snake crawling through the grass, which she is repelled by but refuses to kill because it brings bad luck. This is as close to paradise as he'll ever get, and he watches from the kitchen window as she prunes her plants and weeds the ground around them. She has grown stout in Tampa, but her face, shaded by the large straw hat she wears when she is out in the sun, is still angular and well defined. He can see the sweat moistening the back of her dress. She will take a break soon, come inside, pour herself a glass of water from the clay water pot by which he is standing, and go back to finish her work. Just before noon she comes in for good, her face flushed from the heat and a satisfied look in her eyes. Amadeo will want to make love to her then but will not bring it up, aware after fifteen years of marriage of the special nature of her moods. Neither of them will speak because there is no need. He feels drawn towards her as she is drawn to him by a force akin to gravity which goes beyond the moment and will keep the two of them together for many years despite the days of exhaustion, the days of acrimony, and the days of despair. How long have you been married, people will ask. Fifteen, he will joke, but it feels like one hundred fifty. Julia will give him one of her looks and he will smile at her and shrug his shoulders. He watches as she washes her hands in the sink with a jagged chunk of castile soap and scrubs them with a piece of estropajo until her skin is red. Want some coffee, she asks him and he says yes even though he just had some because this gives them more time together. The tomatoes are almost ready, she says, washing out the water pot. I don't mind them green, he says. I'll cut one up for dinner then. She scoops the coffee from a can into the cloth filter the Cubans call a teta because it tapers to a point and is roughly the shape of a breast. The teta hangs from a stand made of tin under which sits a large metal cup. We're having jaibas. Jaibas, Amadeo says. You have to be careful with them this time of year. Where did you get them? Raul the fishmonger came by early today with a bushel he caught this morning. Did you look at the gills? Yes, and the claws are still snapping. They're in the icebox. Enchilado de jaiba, he says. I invited Padre Alonso. Coño, Amadeo says. That priest is forever getting in the way. That priest is our friend, Amadeo. If it weren't for him Rubén would be in jail. He might as well be, Amadeo says with disgust, and his mood changes in a flash. Ese cura es maricón. That priest is seventy-five years old and worthy of our respect, Julia says. He's never done anything to harm you. That we know of. What do you mean, she asks. She has forgotten about the water and the pot boils over. She takes a kitchen towel and lifts the pot off the stove, pouring the water through the teta. When the coffee is done dripping, she serves two demitasses from the large cup and sits at the table. Rubén has never been the same since he started going over to the parish house for catechism lessons. That is the most ridiculous thing I have ever heard. I won't have you saying those things under my roof. Our roof, mi amor, Amadeo says. Lately, the arguments have been all too frequent. He worries about this, but not enough to stop this one. He swallows his coffee in one gulp and stands. He's an old faggot. Julia throws the kitchen towel on the table and storms out. Amadeo is momentarily satisfied but cannot tell if he has won or lost the argument. No doubt Father Alonso will come tonight, spouting a myriad beatitudes and spoiling Amadeo's dinner and anything else he might have had in mind.

Priests, Amadeo thinks, and is reminded of the one who comes by his room acting like Pope Leo XIII himself and gives him communion, which he takes not out of any sense of devotion but because it allows him to swallow something solid. He cannot recall what happened the day of the jaiba dinner but he remembers the day Father Alonso was run out of town. It was the feast of Saints Peter and Paul, after the schools closed for the year. In those days right after the War of '95 strikes became common in Ibor City, at least one or two a year. There was the Weight-

Scale Strike, the Piece-Work Strike, the Chinchal Strike, and others that had no name and happened simply because workers and management despised each other. Families survived for weeks, sometimes months, on nothing but rice pudding and watery soup. A group of men had gathered outside the Príncipe de Gales factory after a walkout vote Amadeo had led when Pedro Fleitas, a sorter at the Hoyos factory down the street, appeared out of nowhere and said he was on his way to kill the priest. The men sat him down, brought him a glass of water, and when he had settled down they asked him why, to which Pedro Fleitas answered that the priest was conspiring with the owners to undermine the strike. What makes you say that, Amadeo asked. Pedro's right leg shook nervously whenever he spoke. He would stammer at first, then his words came out in a great rush. I . . . I . . . he, Pedro said. He came out of the Martínez Ibor house this morning shaking the hand of Martínez. So what, Amadeo said. He was filled with confidence now that he had won the vote. The other rollers looked up to him. He . . . he . . . Pedro's leg was shaking wildly. He kept trying to steady it with his hand but the limb had a mind of its own. He said at Mass today that it was a mortal sin to go on strike. Amadeo laughed. That would put every cigar worker in Ibor on the straight route to hell. Who listens to priests, anyway? The women, said one of the other men.

My . . . my . . . my, Pedro tried to say. Martica said she won't have sex with me while I'm not working. Maybe now you'll stop having children, someone else said. Pedro had seven children and his wife Martica was pregnant with the eighth. When the men got home that night they realized that Pedro's story was true. Their wives withdrew their intimacies with a determination that bordered on pious fervor. After a week, the men's syndicalist convictions wavered, and after fourteen days the strike fell apart as one by one the workers, including Amadeo himself, lumbered back to work. That was when two of them paid the priest a visit. What was said behind the closed doors of the sacristy, Amadeo never learned. That night someone broke all the stained-glass windows in the church and by morning the priest had packed up his bags and left Ibor. For a while rumors circulated as to where he had gone, but it was not until a year later that he was found dead in a fishing shack on Duck Key. Perhaps Pedro Fleitas finally got to him or the police were right and he had killed himself.

When she heard of Padre Alonso's death, Julia was outraged, claiming the men in the factory had driven the priest crazy. Amadeo was about to say that he got what he deserved but he had a bad headache, like the ones he got when it thundered. He let Julia calm down and changed the conversation to the sow he and Chano were fattening for Christmas. You haven't slaughtered a pig in your life, Julia said. Joaquín the grocer is doing it, Amadeo said, for a bottle of rum. Give him the rum after he kills it, Julia said. Remember when he showed up drunk to kill the González's sow and missed the artery? Amadeo remembers. The pig escaped and ran circles around the neighborhood, spilling its blood and squealing like the devil. Margarito, who lived across the street, tried to shoot it and instead wounded the animal, which only made more blood. It was Noche Buena. Everyone had drunk too much. The pig eventually disappeared into the brush and no one ever found it. Like Padre Alonso, Amadeo thinks. That big sow.

The morning of the stroke Amadeo was wearing his white linen suit, a red tie and tan shoes. On his head he had a brand-new panama hat and on his pinky a gold opal ring he had bought the day he decided never to show his misery to anyone, no matter how willing they might be to show him theirs. It was the first cool day of the fall and he was on his way to the Columbia Restaurant to have his morning coffee and a cigar. He'd sit next to Giacobo Bombo, the mafia boss, and they would talk about game cocks, the situation in Cuba with Carlos Prío, the new president, and other things they were fond of discussing. Never money. Never women. Only young men talk about those things. Then it happened. The first person to come to Amadeo was a street urchin who tried to take his ring, and when he couldn't pull it off, he ran off with his gold watch. The second was a policeman, a relative of Chano whom they called la Bestia for his brute strength and his ruthless treatment of suspected criminals. He tried to lift a limp Amadeo to his feet to no avail. The Beast went in search of help and when he returned, a group had gathered around Amadeo asking him questions which, of course, he could not answer. By that point he knew that he would never move or speak again and that his life was, for all intents and purposes, over. He had gone from one plane of existence to another in a fraction of a second. In one he was healthy and thriving. In the other he was a mound of useless flesh. The Beast dispersed the crowd, which included several friends of Julia from the old days who bent over him trying to gauge the extent of his condition. He heard one of them say, He finally got what he deserved, and he wanted to say back, vieja puta, to the old bitch, but he was glued to the pavement and his throat was rigid like concrete.

Amadeo blinks. Something different about today. The room is filled with amber light. The clown's down-turned mouth seems cheery and the snowy mountains have lost their melancholy air. The dresser on the far wall has the glow of a self-sufficient object. Without it the walls would fall, the window would shatter, the floor would open and Amadeo would be sucked into the center of the earth. Once the drawers held his clothes, brought by his sons on the recommendation of Nurse. It is good, she'd said, for him to have his things near him. He'll feel more at home that way. Not long after, it became obvious that Amadeo would never be leaving his room, that he would never see the objects they had so eagerly placed in the dresser drawers, and that he didn't seem to be responding in any way to the kindness suggested to and acted upon by his officious sons. Even if he'd blinked yes a hundred times, they would not know what he was assenting to. The clothes had grown moldy and stale in their disuse and at some point an attendant had been dispatched to take them away. Now the dresser stands resplendent in its obsolescence. Amadeo cannot tell if he's been awake a long time and he has just fallen asleep or if he has never fallen asleep and this is merely the continuation of an eternal condition from which he will never wake: he and the dresser facing each other but unable to tell each other their stories. Furniture doesn't think. Human beings do. Yet even as he denies the possibility of the dresser thinking, he realizes that Nurse, Nurse II, Orderly, and all the others who look on him have concluded that he is devoid of thought. Just because an object does not exhibit any movement does not mean that it cannot think. It stands to reason that if he is capable of thought so might the dresser be. If the dresser thinks, then, what does it think about? Its emptiness? Its lack of purpose? Does it remember the days when it was full and useful, ready to serve its masters with its bounty of shirts, socks, pajamas, and underwear, hiding in its depths the most important documents, the dearest photographs, the most intimate correspondence? Is it ever content? Does it long for company like Amadeo or lust after Sor Diminuta or Nurse? It is dressed in light veneer and has knobs for handles. Once it had a mirror over it, but they took that away along with his clothes. When does a dresser stop being a dresser? Is it still one even though its drawers are empty of clothes, or is dresserhood independent of functionality? Is he, Amadeo Terra, no longer a human being because he performs no useful function? Presence is essence, Amadeo asserts. Dresser and Amadeo are both present in the room, filled with potential and essential to each other. The dresser affirms him as he affirms the dresser. Outside the room is irrelevant, might as well be another planet, another universe. He and dresser together, forever. The argument is a perfect tautological circle, and if it breaks, consciousness breaks as well. It is the kind of thinking, derived from some obscure philosopher or other, that would make Chano proud.

The only personal item left in the room is a card the nuns sent him for his last birthday. It sits on the far corner of the dresser top where he can see it only if he is resting with his face away from the window. It says Many Blessings on Your Birthday in golden script on a lavender background around a bouquet of wildflowers. The card, when he can see it, reminds him of Julia, who remembered everyone's birthday, especially his, and would prepare a feast of all his favorite foods, perhaps roast a pig if she had the money for it, and have the boys sing him birthday songs. Friends would stop by and drink with him and exchange jokes. There was the one about the lady on the bus who placed a bag of needles on the seat next to her and several about two drunks at the bar and one about the little boy, a friend of Pepito, at school picking his nose and another about a man trying to get a room at a hotel, and many featuring Quevedo. He cannot remember the jokes themselves, only their casings. When he could speak, he didn't have to remember them. They poured out of him one after the other and his friends, unable to contain their laughter, begged him to stop. Julia stood in the background, too modest herself to join the group but smiling nevertheless, and Amadeo made it his challenge to make her laugh, which she would do quietly so no one would notice. Only then would he stop. There were times when he pulled out the domino set, and then the guests stayed until dawn of the following morning. Some struggled home, their heads filled with rum, their pockets heavy with money; others went straight to the factories to make back whatever they had lost.

Amadeo hears a bell ringing down the hall. There comes the beggar, lost in a place of no money. Here is the sybarite, trapped in a place of no pleasure. Fish out of the sea? Bell and a drum. The boy slices the lizard down the belly. What's inside? Mother feeds him soup and stale bread, a real bounty; then he goes to the well for water, cold fresh water from the belly of the earth. The bucket plashes cymbal-like and sound comes floating up like smoke. Water tastes like dream, dream of the ceiba, pig snouting the black earth, dream of his mother in her death throes. Cup of water, heat of afternoon. A breezeless day, like lead, the night in retreat with affliction and relief. At last, he tells himself, I can rest, no longer having to wait on her. Death rattle came, so slight it felt more like an exhalation, a sigh of relief. Mouth stayed open. He pushed the jaw closed and wrapped the head with a handkerchief. Later came the questions from relatives—what was the hour? Run over by a fruit vendor? Where were you? All he wanted was to go far away from her room. Then the call again that never stopped, even from the other side, Amadeo, bring me coffee, followed by the beating of wings, an angel trapped inside a steel cage. Amadeo, bring me my coffee, again and again, he wanting to drown her in coffee. Give me those sweet lips, Amalia. Spread them open like that, like that. In the dream she says yes, I will. In the dream he wants to feel her next to him. Yes, Amalia says, whatever you want. Like butter melting, he thinks waking, and sees the dresser before him resplendent, alive, and he on the bed like a white island. Amalia? Amalia went back to her town to live out the life that lies between hunger and tedium.

Sundays are happy days at Santa Gertrudis. If Nurse is up to it, she will have Orderly move the patients out of their rooms and park them in their chairs or gurneys along the wall. The relatives visiting their nearly departed arrive in the afternoon after lunch and the hall fills with their laughter and their condescending talk. Usually there is at least one birthday to celebrate and the kin will bring balloons, paper hats and a cake, which the patients, those who still have stomachs, will be allowed to taste. Today is not unusual. Someone on the other end of the floor has survived yet another year and the family, loud Cubans all, have come not just with cake but with black beans and rice, pork, fried plantains, and a bottle of rum. Several of the children are chasing each other and running in and out of the patients. A small girl with pigtails hides behind Amadeo's chair and when one of the bigger boys finds her, he pushes the chair out of the way and nearly topples Amadeo over. Nurse and Orderly are too involved with the party to notice. Nurse is holding a huge plate of food while Orderly is drinking out of a plastic cup normally used to give patients their medicine. Amadeo's mouth starts to water and he is desperately trying to keep from drooling. He can smell the food and he can taste the rum. Someone is playing a guitar and singing and a man with a thick black mustache is pouring another round of drinks. If they would only get closer, if they would only let him taste, if he could only get up and dance with the little girl. Next to him is a woman with a smile on her face. She seems frozen in a state of permanent joy. Her eyes are closed and she is taking short deep breaths as if she were about to start hiccuping. Across from him is a man wearing a hunting cap. He is standing motionless with arms at his sides waiting for a bus, it seems. The lady who calls out for Mari is nowhere to be seen or heard. As the relatives of the other patients come and go they look with concern to the end of the hall where the party is in full swing. Some grumble under their breath and whisper to their companions, Don't they realize this is a place of rest, who do they think they are, when in fact the last thing their relatives need is rest. They don't dare approach the Cubans, Amadeo is convinced, because they think that loud people are by nature aggressive. Instead they stand next to their parents or grandparents and speak to them in gay tones that mask an almost palpable anxiety. Suddenly a young woman whom he doesn't recognize is standing in front of him. He has not received a family visitor since Rubén came with his wife and spent the whole time talking about a poet Amadeo had never heard of, Carlos Williams, what kind of mixed-up name is that. The young woman has a heart-shaped face and dreamy black eyes. She speaks to him in Spanish in a voice so sweetly tempered and graceful he is reminded of Julia. There is nothing like the sweetness of the Cuban woman. He thinks this in English but he means *la dulzura,* a quality that is so hard to describe in English because it is so sorely lacking in the women here. As naturally as she has started speaking, the young woman wipes the drool from his face with a birthday napkin and begins to feed him cake. It has real whipped-cream frosting and is as soft and moist as he has ever tasted. It is filled in the middle with guava jelly of the homemade kind, he can tell. All he needs to do is press his mandibles together several times and the thing dissolves in his mouth in such a festival of taste that his eyes water. The young woman is saying that he reminds her of her uncle. Does your uncle think about tasting you when he eats cake?

Amadeo's diarrhea starts later that afternoon after all the visitors have gone home and he is back in his room watching the sunset through the slatted window. It begins with the usual drum roll in his intestines, but this time there is no revolution, just a slow release like a river flooding vast surrounding areas with silt and mud until all you can see are the tops of trees. That is the first movement. Two hours later there are bombs bursting, a trepidation of trumpets, a fanfare of farting, and a deflation of his bowels accompanied by odors so overpowering they make him gag. He cannot believe there is so much sulfurous rot inside him, he cannot believe how much pestilence, how much base matter, liquid and pervasive, is coming out of him. If someone were to walk into the room they would think Amadeo has just returned from hell. Nurse II will not be by until midnight and so he must lie in the fetid pool of his own wastes barely able to breathe. He calms himself down with the thought that it is better it all come out of him now than in the morning when Nurse returns. The third movement is a dam bursting, a huge wave of brown water sluicing through a valley taking everything with it—houses, trees, whole mountains—leaving behind it total devastation and the quiet of the grave. There is no smell with this one. Amadeo is exhausted and he falls asleep clinging to the depleted island of his own body. When Nurse II comes in at around 12:30 she says Dios mío with such distress that it wakes Amadeo. Nurse II, usually all business when she washes him, keeps saying Ay, ay, under her breath and turns her face away when it comes time to wipe him. Before leaving she sprays room deodorizer over Amadeo and says a final Dios mío as she turns off the lights.

He imagines himself laughing right now, loudly, up-roariously. An ocean of shit has just come out of him, all the result of a little cake in the afternoon, fed to him by a beautiful young woman who had only his happiness in mind. Happiness in mind. That's what he feels. Empty, dehydrated, floating in midair like a balloon over the bed, over the hospital, over the city, over the sea, next to the soaring black birds with the scissor tails. From here he can see everything—the fishermen on their boats, swimmers on the beach. He can look down on the street where he lived, his last house set back on a corner lot. He can float over la casita that Julia fixed, where the boys became men, and the Príncipe de Gales factory where he worked. Close by is Casa Cuba and the Centro Asturiano. The people there are strangers to him. All his friends are dead, his sons spread throughout the country. Amadeo is no longer floating but back on his bed, Julia standing at the foot, hair loose and disheveled. He wants to tell her to fix herself, he doesn't like to see her like that. He wants to say she should change her dress for one more becoming. He wants to ask why she's so pale. I've been waiting for you, he says, which is as close as he can come to affection. He asks about Albertico, but as much as he wants to hear her voice she won't respond because she is a figment of his imagination, a specter released from his mind in the middle of the sordid night. One blink and she's gone. Alina, the daughter he had with Amalia, appears in her place. She has the face of the woman who fed him cake and turned his entrails inside out. She is smiling and offers him a spoonful of cake. Move to the side of the bed, he wants to say, and she does. Just as the spoon is inches away from his mouth, she drops it on the bed and it rolls off his body to the floor.

Alone in the dead morning hours Amadeo is over-powered by longing—ansia is the Spanish word that first comes to his mind—for all that has rolled off him to the ground beyond his reach: cake, Julia, island, past. He is looking out the window of his childhood to the road that passed by there, red and rutted by the wheels of cane wagons. The sun is setting over the mango trees across the way and off in the distance the hills have turned a hazy blue. The birds have stopped singing and the cocuyos are flying about, their green lights going on and off. He hears the baying of his father's pack mule, the snorting of the pigs in the sty, and his mother's voice riding over, Muchacho, get away from the evening air—el sereno, she called it—before it enters you and ruins your blood. Amadeo is waiting for his father to come home riding his sorrel mare, whistling a guajira if he is in a good mood or silent if he's not, which means Amadeo will have to hide until he goes to sleep. Get away, muchacho, his mother says again. Who are you waiting for every night? For him. Amadeo hears the first owl cooing over the house. When the night comes it will be so dark he will not be able to see his hand in front of his face. Then he will be safe. His mother goes on doing whatever she does in the back room singing her song, Y cuando te veo pasar, se me pone el alma tan fría que voy corriendo a la mar para ponerme tranquila. Bang, he wants to shoot his father. Bang, bang. His mother was a dark woman with faraway eyes. She cared nothing for the new world her husband brought her to. He is a monument to death, your father is, and his voice is the echo of the sea, the deepest grave.

Amadeo wants the cake and his mother's hand and his father's voice. He wants his boyhood in the country, he wants the city that made him a man, he wants that man he was when he first met Julia. He wants the sea, wants to be island and salt water, wants to be the city that braves the waves. Ansia, slow return of what he lost and didn't know he had. In him now, the sweet smoke of absence. Out of him so, tobacco and the island. Chano once told him: Abandon what you want and you will find it in you. That was after the cigar factory burned down and the land on which it stood smoldered for weeks afterward. What Chano meant then, Amadeo thinks, is that his desire is his making. He is the sea, he is the island and water and city, he is the women he loved, beer he drank, cake he ate, cigars he made. Man he was then, man he is now. When Amadeo found him in the arms of one of the girls at La Matancera, Chano said, Loving her I love myself, then had a drink of rum. Why do you gamble if you do not want for money, Amadeo asked him once at a card game. Everyone in town knew the game was fixed. Only fools played there. Money is my monkey, Chano said. I make it dance, it makes me dance. What is your monkey, Amadeo? Amadeo wanted to answer cigars but he had developed a temporary allergy on his hands that made them crack and swell with blisters. Doctor told him he had to change professions. For a long time he pondered the question and then he thought he found the answer when the War of '95 broke out. He joined the PRC, Martí's party, volunteered as a mambí and was sent to a training camp in Ocala for six weeks. When he returned Julia was beside herself. Men playing war, she said over and over again, men playing war while their families starve. The expeditionary force, much smaller than anticipated due to financial problems, left without Amadeo. Martí was killed a few weeks later in Oriente. Amadeo, whose hands had gotten better and whose money kept getting smaller by the day, went back to his cigar rolling and waited patiently to be called up, urging his fellow cigar workers to support the cause with money and provisions. He drove Julia crazy with the Friday night meetings he held in their living room and risked having the house raided by police for hiding weapons and munitions for the revolutionaries. In '98 the United States joined the war against Spain and the thing was over in a few months. Amadeo's disappointment was such that he took $1,000 he was holding for the PRC, rushed to the cockfights and lost half; then he went to La Matancera and spent the rest on cheap rum and cheap whores. When he returned home, Julia had dinner ready for him. Everything was as it had been before.

The bell is not beggar or sybarite but priest. He is coming down the hall offering communion to the patients, accompanied by a dwarf dressed in cassock and surplice who rings the brass bell and who suffers from elephantiasis of the testicles. Amadeo doesn't know this, but Chano once told him of this horrifying ailment and now Amadeo is determined to apply this diagnosis to the dwarf. Otherwise, why does he walk with his legs spread out like so? Of course, most of the patients have not the wherewithal to accept or decline the flesh of Jesus Christ. They lie on their beds or sit on their chairs staring at the nothingness, or, in Amadeo's particular case, at a wood veneer dresser. If their mouths are open, the priest will simply place the host on their tongues as he does every morning in church, oblivious to what harm it may cause once it is swallowed. If their mouths are closed, he will have the dwarf, who has a hand like an industrial vise, press on their mandibles until they part. Amadeo knows the drill all too well so that by the time the priest and his helper reach his room, the bell so loud it seems death is at hand, Amadeo's mouth is open to take in the thin round wafer that he will attempt to savor with every one of the taste buds that remain on his tongue. Because his room is the last one on the floor, the priest will often sit on the visitor's chair by the door and rest, taking a handkerchief out of his pocket to wipe his forehead and asking the dwarf, who never seems to say a word, to get him a cool glass of water from the nurse. The priest is a youngish man with a broad forehead and small ears that swoop outward from his face. He sits with his back perfectly straight. Today the dwarf returns balancing a glass of water on one hand and, on the other, a cup of coffee much of which has spilled onto the saucer. Thank you, Rigo, you are a saint. The priest removes the stole and drapes it over Rigo's shoulders. The dwarf smiles at Amadeo who can barely see him from the corner of his eye. He can't tell who the real freak is, or if all three of them are. Consider yourself fortunate, Rigo, the priest says motioning to Amadeo, that you are not in his condition, unable to speak or move or even think. This man's life has been reduced to the simplest essence, and it is in that fashion that God loves him: simply, essentially. This last statement annoys Amadeo. It should be obvious to the priest and everyone else who enters his room that he is as full of life as the next fellow. Let us pray for him, Rigo, that God may see fit to take him out of his misery. Misery, Amadeo thinks. He never thought of himself as miserable. He wants to hit the priest, send him flying back to his church. To add insult to injury the dwarf walks over to Amadeo's leather chair by the window, climbs onto it, and sits, his legs hanging from the edge. Amadeo blinks no repeatedly; then he begins to drool and fart with rage. Look, Rigo, the priest says in a sanctimonious tone, the poor man is having a fit. Get the nurse and I will stay here and pray. When the dwarf returns with Nurse in tow, a froth of spittle has formed on Amadeo's lips. Nurse turns to the priest and says that he should not be concerned about Mr. Terra. He is a problem patient, he will not cooperate, he drools and messes himself constantly. If I could cooperate I would, Amadeo thinks. If I could walk out of here, I would. The priest looks up to Nurse who looms over him like a fleshy Matterhorn. He stands with some difficulty, for Nurse has not given him enough space to maneuver himself out of the chair; then he goes over to the bed, mumbles a Latin prayer that Amadeo cannot understand, and makes the sign of the cross over him. He retrieves the stole from Rigo's shoulders, shakes his head and thanks Nurse for the coffee. As he is leaving, Amadeo farts and Nurse gives him an annoyed look.

Julia has come in from the garden with a plate of red and green tomatoes, which she places on the kitchen table. She picks a red one and slices it with the large knife she brought from Cuba. The blade, worn from so much sharpening, cuts through the tomato as if it were butter. Julia arranges the slices on a plate and dresses them with salt and olive oil. She places the plate and a loaf of Cuban bread between her and Amadeo. Amadeo tears the loaf in two and hands half to Julia. He splits the other open with his thumbs and makes a sandwich with several tomato slices. As he eats he watches Julia do the same thing. She eats heartily but gracefully and in between bites says that the tomatoes are good this year. At one point red juice dribbles out of the side of her mouth, which she wipes with her apron. Her fingers are long and delicate but she holds the bread firmly and a few crumbs drop on the tablecloth. She picks them up by pressing down on them with her index finger, which she then takes to her mouth and licks. Amadeo likes to watch her eat in these moments when they are by themselves, wanting them to stretch out the length of the afternoon but they never do. One of the children comes into the kitchen wanting something from their mother or a neighbor stops by with a bit of gossip, or one of the cigar workers appears unexpectedly with news about a union matter. He gets up from the table and lights a cigar, the smoke clouding his face, and makes a comment that will return the broken world to the space between them—you planted too much calabaza this year, you are gaining too much weight. It is his father in him, gulping and spewing smoke like a belching dragon. If I am disappointed, let the world be disappointed with me.

Whenever he leaves the house on one of his walks it is Havana, not Tampa, he wants around him. At dusk, muted in a smoky light, he goes back to it, remembering a balcony on Reina Street where a girl with long brown hair eats guava paste and looks down the street at nothing in particular; or O'Reilly where an old man in rags is praising God and cursing Spaniards; or the Paseo del Prado where a band is playing danzas in the new style. It is the memory of his father whipping him that enters his heart like a burning needle and stays there turning end over end. He shuts that door, then Havana turns back into Tampa and he is walking down Séptima. He should return, find a woman there who will understand him like Julia did before Albertico died and their lives went to hell; then he hears the drip of the bathroom faucet and realizes where he is. Drip, drip into the sink all night and he trying to sleep, erase the burning needle. Fear has driven him every day of his life. He shuts that door. Drunk and asleep on a whore's bed, shut that. Waking on a park bench at dawn and showing up at the factory where the foreman laughs at him and sends him home. Standing before Julia, bleary-eyed and odorous, asking her forgiveness. She serves him a plate of vaca frita and slices of avocado, which he eats alone. Albertico's limp arm hanging down. Shut that, shut that. He has been living his life over and over, every step, every dark corner, the interstices, the voids. Julia tells him she is going back to the island to live the rest of her life in peace. There is no anger in her voice, there is no love. Bang, he shoots his father again. Bang, in the back of the head. He hears of Julia's death and the needle goes deeper. Everything happens in the present, all around him simultaneously. Who says he cannot feel? What do the doctors know?

Each drop of the faucet punctuates his condition, each is a measure of his helplessness. Once he was a man who worked, who smoked, who fixed leaks. Once he thought of death as a silent far-off place that had nothing to do with him. Now death is the sound of the faucet dripping (Chano would enjoy that one), a man hanging, his wife screaming cabrón, hijo de puta. A fourteen-year-old is a woman, he says to Julia. A fourteen-year-old doesn't play with dolls. A man has certain needs. That I can't satisfy? That you can't satisfy. How could I marry you, she says, her face twisted with regret. You did. Mal rayo te parta, she says. Amadeo pushes her out of the way and goes outside to smoke. Evil lightning has broken him. The curse came true even if it took a long time. Shut that door. He hears one slow drip followed by two quick ones and then a ping in his chest. Just as he is getting used to the room, the quiet when Nurse is not present, the sun blinking through the window, the pastels of the sea outside so blue, so endocrine, and the radio playing music in the hall, Nurse II singing along, just as he has, at long last, put out the fire of his past and accepted this room as his world, which he will live in forever until forever ends, comes the drip, drip drip, drip, drip drip, a beat no one can dance to unless he's limp and holding a cane. Each drip is the name of someone he knew: Alfibio, Sagrada, Heriberto, Manolo, Israel, Saelo, Bermudo, Anastasio, Nelia, Eduviges, Elvina, Seferino, Tania, Samara, Longino, Cresencio, Aurelio, Carmela, Domingo, Alejandro, Pancracia, Filio, Darminia, Dolores, Esencia, Apolonio, Mateo, Germán, Sonora, Martirio. All the re-membering is keeping him awake when he should be learning the art of forgetting. He remembers the storm that broke the cathedral's belfry. He remembers a dog licking its broken leg, Ana's sweet untouched face, his mother's breath, Julia's purple nipples, a man beating his horse with a two-by-four, a rumbero levitating over his drums, the face of a man who fell dead in a cockfight, he remembers the imaginary beach of his lack of ambi-tion, a fish jumping out of the water into an imaginary sky, the waves slinking in, bringing messages from another imaginary beach where the moon is licking his hand and a lone sentinel stands guard. Amadeo remembers food, numbers, addresses, sighs, angers, the fierce green of his country, a man there in the distance riding a sorrel mare. He confuses places and names, he mixes up times and dates. In one memory he kills his son; in another he is bouncing him on his knee. He remembers Tavito his brother: toy enamorao como la hoja el caimito. He is laughing, he is crying, he has just bought Julia a diamond ring. He remembers songs and small white waves breaking on a black beach, Amalia's belly, Alina's hair, black clouds over cane fields, his father's red face. Albertico, Albertico, shut that door.

An eternity he listens to all that he'd like to forget until Nurse II notices the leak and sends in a plumber. He is ruddy and bulbous with whiskers growing out of his nose. He is speaking to himself in the bathroom and complains about the plumbing in Santa Gertrudis, heaping curses and condemnations so vile that even Amadeo holds his breath. Amadeo listens with interest: he hears the banging and clanging of the tools on the metal pipes, the plumber's deep breathing, the scuff of his work boots on the tile floor. After an hour the plumber comes back out. He pulls a red handkerchief out of his back pocket to wipe his face. The faucet stems were totally stripped. I replaced both and put on new washers. You have a good faucet there for many years, he says to Amadeo. The man is standing at the foot of the bed expecting a response. All Amadeo can do is stare back. Cat swallow your tongue? the plumber says. Cocksucker can't talk. Can you move? Holy fucking shit. Can you hear?

You're in sad shape, my friend, mi amigo. The men are staring at each other in silence. The plumber is frozen in space holding the handkerchief next to his face. Amadeo blinks. You can hear, says the plumber. Amadeo blinks yes again. Amadeo would like the plumber to stay, blink. Amadeo would like him to tell Nurse II, blink. His mind works, his thoughts work, blink, blink. Tell about the leak, tell me how you fixed it, blink, blink. I was walking down the street, blink, and all of a sudden, blink. The people here don't know anything, blink. They think I'm a vegetable, blink, blink, blink, blink. The plumber finishes wiping his neck and face and puts the handkerchief away. Amadeo is blinking fiercely, trying to make a language the plumber will understand. The plumber is looking at him strangely, he stammers a phrase Amadeo cannot make out, then he composes himself. Well, he says, I fixed your faucet, friend, and leaves. Amadeo's eyes are burning. He has communicated with someone for the first time in almost five years but he has left the room and will, most likely, never return. He is not disappointed and he is not overwhelmed with desperation. Rather, he feels buoyant, a physical lightness that makes him close his eyes and rest, sunlight warming the room, the conversation between Nurse II and the plumber in the hall barely audible over the happy purr of his body.

★   ★   ★

Two, three times a year the volunteer ladies bring flowers to him that the local florist donates to Santa Gertrudis. He can smell them from where he lies, especially the ones like him that are close to death, and they trigger the memories of the garden, and of Julia in it, like a flower herself out of whom emanates the scent of paradise gained. But paradise is not, Amadeo knows, here in this room. This is hell because he cannot leave it, this is hell because it is the smell of death that reaches his nostrils—the flowers, himself. No use thinking there might be another chance (an exception made just for him) hidden away in the files of the laws of the physical universe. Santa Gertrudis teaches you otherwise, no delusions allowed. If he is alive it is only because his sons are paying for him to be fed, washed, and cured when he needs curing. It is their money he should be cursing, money that keeps him from the total forgetfulness death will bring. This is a realization that should cause him great consternation, but it does not. A garden has insects, a forest has beasts, a sky has birds, Santa Gertrudis has patients, nurses, Amadeo, blink blink, blink blink blink.

The cigar smoke is filling Amadeo's mouth. He holds it there, shaping it with his mouth, chewing on it to get the full taste before letting it float out. It is a Sunday morning and there is nowhere he needs to be. Julia has cut several of the yellow roses which she will trim and place in a vase in the living room. She is now digging a trench along the far wall behind the outhouse and handles the pickax with the strength and confidence of a man, Amadeo thinks, then corrects himself. There is nothing masculine about her. He holds the cigar in front of him and studies it. The ash is a light gray and it burns evenly around. The taste is even and the smoke doesn't bite. The vein of the wrapper leaf curls to the left, as it should. He knows not to roll the wrapper too tightly for that will make the cigar not draw right. The smoke is moist but doesn't have the moldy taste of tobacco that has lain too long in the ship's hold. In short, he is smoking as perfect a cigar as can be made in an imperfect world. Last night she told him she was thinking of planting a grapevine along the far fence. You've never planted grapes before in your life, he said. Time to start, she said. They won't grow in this climate, he said. How do you know, she said. Too hot, the vine won't yield fruit. Then we'll have an arbor we can sit under. She planted the vine and it grew and gave fruit, small bitter grapes not even the birds ate, but it gave good shade and made the backyard usable during the hottest months. Amadeo and Chano spent many a Sunday afternoon under the arbor smoking and talking.

It was there that Amadeo first heard about Spinoza, a Portuguese Jew who practiced philosophy in Amsterdam, and Dostoevski, the greatest writer of all time according to Chano, and Shakespeare, who could make poetry out of belching, and Voltaire who had no hair on his tongue. It was no secret that Chano was a walking encyclopedia, but few people knew that he was a secret poet and penned many poems that he recited to Amadeo while they sat under the arbor smoking and drinking. Amadeo remembers one in which he compared a vagina to the rising sun and another in which a tree trunk drips sap while pining for a lost love and a third about a flea that bites two lovers and thus causes their blood to unite. Amadeo argued with him that in these parts a mosquito would be a more appropriate insect to use in a poem of that sort, and Chano said he had thought of a flea first and that is what made its way into the poem. Easy to criticize the poet after the fact, he argued, but at the moment of creation he must utilize not what is proper but what is there. He never admitted to Amadeo that he had stolen his idea from a long-dead English poet who would never have written a poem about a barbaric mosquito rather than a fanciful flea.

Amadeo longs for those days when all he needed was to sit in the shade with a bottle of wine, a cigar, and a friend or two to feel like the king of the universe. Better yet if they were playing dominoes, shouting out numbers as they slammed the pieces on the table. He remembers Ordóñez the Spaniard who got up and ran around the table when he dominated with the capicúa and Delfín Morales, smug and self-reliant, who thought three moves ahead as if he were playing chess and would regale the group with stories of high-stakes games he had played in Havana. In one a lawyer lost a twenty-room house he had just built for his wife, and in another a sugar magnate who lost all his cash tried to wager his no-good homosexual son. I made millions, Morales said, and lost them all again. Amadeo, pass me the rum, and he would pour himself a glass which he would drink in one gulp. No matter how much he drank he always won and never left the table before the losers. I learned my domino manners in La Plaza del Vapor where you could get knifed for looking at a man the wrong way. The day he stopped coming to Amadeo's backyard a certain legitimacy left with him and the games were not the same. Julia liked Morales less than she liked Chano and thought him a rogue. She was right, of course, but Amadeo admired Delfín Morales as much as he admired Chano, the latter because of his intelligence, the former because he had taken the money of powerful men and had seen them crumble afterwards. He died in a village north of Tarpon Springs, shot in the back by a man whose woman he stole.

Amadeo hears the bell again. This time it sounds dull, off key. Someone's died. The last thing he needs is a priest, especially one with the rod of sanctimony stuck up his ass, and is relieved to hear the bell pass by and the clanging recede down the hall. Time was he didn't care what the priest did to him. Time was he didn't care about anything and just wanted to be out of Santa Gertrudis. He is afraid of the priest and wants nothing to do with him. God doesn't speak, God doesn't meddle in human affairs. That's what Spinoza said, according to Chano. God doesn't care about Amadeo and Amadeo doesn't care about God. Tomorrow he may be shivering in a soulless despair but today Amadeo has simply reached the conclusion that believing in God is like believing in the unknown. Julia, he'd rather believe in Julia. Leave it at that.

Amadeo doesn't know what language he is thinking in. Sometimes it is Spanish, sometimes English; sometimes it feels like no language at all. Nurse has come and fed him breakfast and talked to him of the weather—the first cool day in months and the clouds moving along, one puff after another, a herd of clouds, a herd of puffs like thoughts across the sky. Nurse says, he thinks she says, that her boyfriend is waiting for her after work. They are going to a picnic by the bay. Nurse has a boyfriend—tiene novio—and Amadeo is astounded at the thought. The clouds, the romantic picnic on the bay, Nurse and her boyfriend, life outside Santa Gertrudis, everything conspires in favor of English. Not that he cares. Spanish flies away like a sheet of onionskin paper, papel de china, and disappears to the south. Nurse's voice is a register higher than usual, giddy, anticipating. She tells him that they are bringing their dog, a bull terrier with a black patch around the left eye. His name is Bull's Eye and he is mean from being tied up all day, but once you let him loose, he runs back and forth across the grass, he chews up sticks; sometimes he jumps in the water and swims around in a big circle. Amadeo blinks in his own impenetrable language as she swirls the spoon inside the baby food jar to get the last of the liver and onion paste she is feeding him. I'm making meat loaf sandwiches from last night's leftovers and potato salad. Jackson is bringing beer and his guitar. He plays in a band, you know. Amadeo wants to tell her that his oldest son used to play guitar, too. He was so good people thought he should turn professional. Then he went to New York. By the time I saw him again he had given up his guitar and had picked up some new habits: the habit of dress, the habit of drink, and the habit of poetry. Amadeo has not seen his son—what is his name?—in a long time. Rubén, Rubén, that's the name. He sent him a book he published, which didn't make sense to Amadeo. It was dedicated, For Papi, that he should feel proud, but he did not feel proud. He felt confused and embarrassed. The poems didn't even rhyme. Nurse is feeding him peach and is involved in her own talk about the picnic: The last time they went Jackson brought his fishing pole and caught a large sting ray he didn't know what to do with once he pulled it ashore. Later on in the afternoon it thundered and rained and they packed their things and got drenched running the few steps to the parking lot. It is an engrossing story for the simple reason that it makes Amadeo realize Nurse is sometimes more than Nurse—lover, dog owner, cook. Amadeo is waiting for his last spoonful and he can't swallow fast enough to keep saliva from filling his mouth. It is not mango but lowly peach. Peach is ten times better than pear or prune. Pear is wet sand. Prune is mud. Nurse is lady mango and today is her day in the sun, swimming in mango sea, dripping with mango juice, making mango jam. She and her man will catch fish tonight, drink some beer, let their dog run free. They will go home and put a record on the phonograph, do a little dancing in the living room. Nurse will be out of her uniform and maybe she will look sexy. Jackson will kiss her meaty lips, move his hand up and down her back as they dance, and big oceanic Nurse, with thighs like whales, will be slurping back and wanting more. And those two beasts will grind against each other like mountains, like fleshy glaciers, like masses of clouds that form over the ocean in late afternoon and surge upwards in columns until they burst into great down-pours of thunder and rain. Amadeo takes the last of the peach in his mouth, sees Nurse looming over him with a smile like a river, like a traffic light, like a big slice of mango in the white sky of her face.

Today the lady across the way is quiet. Garrido has not come inquiring about his shoelaces in several days. Not even Orderly's voice, which usually echoes through the hall all day long, is audible, and Amadeo is waiting for someone to puncture the silence of the early morning when he hears a familiar voice from the past. A chicken waddles by. He smells the backyard, hears a rooster crowing. The dog Campana is trying to catch flies with his mouth. He hears the voice again. Outside clouds have gathered, not the white billowing ones but thick leaden masses. Morning like dusk. The voice again followed by thunder, Julia entering through the door, hair and clothes wet, catching her breath, screaming that lightning has struck the Gales factory. Amadeo struggles to put his pants on, a shirt, no shoes, then runs outside, the thick heavy drops hitting his face and lightning striking all around him, the ozone smell, large puddles on the sandy roads, the factory on fire, fire-men, pumps, hoses, flames spewing through the shattered windows, black smoke rising into the rain, people huddled in clusters, the workers trapped inside burned alive, then a woman being restrained. She wants to rush into the building, into the flames. Back home in the kitchen, he has a drink of rum to warm up and listens to Julia list the dead while she cooks a pot of soup that she will take to the widows: Arsenio and Wilfredo Gómez, José Benítez, Catarino López, el Curro Vergara, el chino Chan, Elpidio Vázquez, Rafaelito Sáenz, on and on and goes beyond the twenty trapped in the factory and invokes people who didn't die then but later of sickness or accident or old age. Amadeo hears the names of all the dead he has known but one and she is about to say it when he blinks and she's gone.

The morning draws itself out and lengthens into a flat expanse of light where Amadeo feels shunted, bleached, diminished. Havana, he thinks, mornings in Havana were not like this. There was hot sun, there was the smell of fruit in the market, there were street hawkers singing their wares and women calling to them from the balconies and flowers dripping down the verandahs. There were stores open to the street and big black men carting bundles of cotton, sacks of sugar, baskets of fish. The arcades were filled with people who were alive, yelling and laughing, cursing one another then laughing again, for that is the way Cubans end things, with laughter. There were bookstores and shoe stores, pharmacies and lottery booths and newspapers of every type; there were ladies in their finery and

Spanish soldiers and creole scribes and mulatto shoe shiners and Chinese cooks. Carts went by with fruit and vegetables, sides of beef, whole pigs slaughtered that very morning. There were huge hotels and small bars where you could sit and drink and not be bothered. There were street musicians and magicians and all manner of entertainment to be had for pennies. There were Hungarians, Filipinos, Englishmen, Irish boys and French matrons and American businessmen and Jewish peddlers. There were small alleyways to visit at night and broad tree-shaded promenades filled with Sunday strollers, children chasing each other, vendors selling peanuts, pork sandwiches, churros, coffee, sugar cane juice, fresh coconut that they would cut open on the sidewalk with a huge machete. On the Prado large black men dressed in white stood at the corners watching the traffic pass and small white men dressed in black played brisca, the Spanish card game, under the almond trees. Delight in disorder, the poet called it. That's what Havana was. Amadeo wants to laugh, he is filled to bursting with that city, he wants to laugh away what has happened to him. Then all is gone in a wisp of smoke, Havana smoke.

He remembers how things between him and Julia thinned, then broke. She went to her rosary and her children; he went to Amalia's dark belly, her big laugh like a mare in heat, her loamy smell. Albertico was dead and Amadeo could not stay in the house without thinking of him, his little nonsense games, his races from the living room to the kitchen. Julia abandoned him for a peculiar holiness, set herself up as a curandera to whom people came—at first only women, eventually men as well. Oh my wayward son, oh my adulterous husband, oh my dying mother. She held her sessions in the kitchen on a tall oak chair Jacobo Azar the carpenter designed especially so she could sit high over the supplicants. She dressed in flowing white or red or blue tunics depending on the day of the week and the saint she wanted to invoke. The neighbors passed by into the kitchen, one by one at first—Fefe from across the street, Carla Delgado, the pharmacist's wife, Fico el cojo, doña Cándida Cadenas, the wealthiest woman in Ibor—then they came in groups from as far away as Ocala and Sarasota. People milled about on the porch, sat on Amadeo's chair, and fell asleep on the sofa while waiting for their consultation with Julia, who sat on her chair like a high priestess barely blinking and declaring her pronouncements with a tubular voice and an accent that sounded like a Cuban version of an ancient European sage. Amadeo thought for sure his wife had lost her mind. At night after the crowds left, she had visions of the spirit world and held long conversations with the Virgin of Charity about the troublesome future of the human race. One night as Amadeo got ready for bed, Julia called him from the bathroom they had installed the week before and said, Amadeo, I have only six months to live. I am going to Havana to die. Amadeo went into the bathroom and saw her sitting on the toilet staring at the wall. You look fine to me, he said. The Virgin told me. She is ordering me to go back so that I can free my spirit over the waters. Go then, he said. He was sick of the pervasive sadness of the house and of Julia's craziness. She went and did not die in the six months the Virgin had predicted but lasted two years. When he found out about her death, he wandered the city for a month feeling betrayed and hopeless, with the elephant of grief sitting on his shoulders.

Julia enters the room and sits on the visitor's chair under the picture of the craggy mountains. She is Julia before the santería and the lunacy, before the long flow-ing robes of a high priestess, radiant with the long Semitic hair of her ancestors. She has a birth mark at the edge of her lower lip and that look of certainty in her eyes, as if she knows his thoughts before he says them. If Amadeo were a woman, he would like to be Julia. The craziness, Amadeo thinks, was only a means of understanding a world that kept taking things away from her. The lace and cot-ton dress she is wearing covers her chest and is pinned at the neck with a cameo brooch. It's been such a long time, he says. Julia smiles and her face fills with light. I was away, she says. I don't like this place, Julia de mi vida. You've never liked any place. The boys put me here. Leave, then. I can't. Yes, you can. I will help you. She comes around the side of the bed and takes him by the arm. With her help he is able to sit up. He swings his legs to the floor, lurches forward and stands. Straightening up is a slow process which he does in increments, for all the years lying down have softened his spine; then he looks down to see the mound of his belly covered with a white hospital gown and below that an erection pointing straight out. Hah! He looks up to meet her eyes. He has forgotten their color and is pleased to see them a greenish blue. Turn, she says, and he does. Walk, she says, and he obeys, placing one awkward foot in front of the other, inching forward around the bed and out the door. They shuffle down the hallway ablaze in morning light, a fat old man helped along by a young woman dressed in a beautiful lace dress. He can smell her lilac smell, he can feel her long fingers holding up his arms. They take the elevator to the first floor, walk outside onto the grass in front of the driveway. His bare feet, gnarled and lumpy from disuse, seem like large unearthly worms marooned in chlorophyll. A sudden breeze catches his hair, and lifts it gently off his head as if her fingers were running through it. Time ago the future was this simple. Time ago there was a future.

Amadeo runs away from school. He hides in the mango grove where he eats fruit and talks with the lizards all day. When Amadeo's father is not tending his fields or stocking the counters at the store, he is angry at the salesmen who try to sell him short, at his customers who haven't paid their bills, at the weather when it rains too much or not enough, at his wife because the food she cooked gives him heart-burn, at Amadeo for hiding in the grove. He will explode one day. Amadeo knows from an early age to avoid his father. Better the midday heat in the grove, better the sweet smell of rotting mangoes. The lizards know well before the father appears that he is looking for Amadeo with a switch in his hand. They splay themselves out and expand their red throats so that Amadeo has enough time to climb up a tree from where he can watch the old man walk angrily around waving the chucho, calling out cabrón, hijo de puta, come out. After some time he tires, his face red as the Canary sun he was born under, and goes back to the house to drink the thick Spanish wine that will kill him before he is fifty. Amadeo comes down just in time to talk with the snakes that lie curled at the base of the tree. The snakes are afraid of the moon and dogs and people but they do not mind

Amadeo, who hates spiders and kills them so the snakes can eat them. The snakes tell Amadeo that he should leave his house as soon as he can, that the world is not full of rage and fear and bitter Spaniards. They warn him never to take fruit from a woman. Amadeo likes their dark green color but he dares not touch them. Then there is a rustling behind a coffee bush and he thinks his father has come back to fetch him and he starts to climb back up the tree, but it is his brother Tavito who has found him and starts honking like a goose. He talks as if he had no mouth and the words came out through his nose. Amadeo barely understands what his brother is saying, something about being in love, about getting married. There is a red welt running across his forearm, where his father has hit him. According to their mother, Tavito is retarded because he drank water from the fountain, which is her way of saying that as he was being born he opened his mouth and inhaled the fluid of the womb. Amadeo tells Tavito to be quiet and pulls him down by the arm to where he sits against the trunk. Tavito obeys his brother and whispers his honks, Toy enamorao como la hoja el caimito, he says repeatedly hitting his forehead with his knuckles. Toy enamorao como la hoja el caimito. By the time Tavito quiets down it is dusk. The sky is orange on one side and dark blue on the other. The snakes have slithered away and Amadeo decides it is safe to return to the house. His father is asleep from all the wine and by tomorrow he will supplant his anger with work. His father is Amadeo's darkness.

It rains for many days and nights. It is a weighty rain, falling straight down, and if you go into it, it sears you. You feel every drop cutting into your skin, drumming on your skull, making it impossible to breathe. Morning is like night and night is a deep place from which no one ever returns. All the animals want to come inside the house and Amadeo's mother spends her time shooing them back out. At first it is the black pigs that live in the yard; next, the chickens try to sneak into the kitchen when her back is turned. Even the bullfrogs that live around the watering trough have had enough rain. Amadeo's father catches them in the bedroom and cuts off their legs, then throws their torsos into the mud of the yard while they are still alive. He cooks the legs in lard and feeds them to the boys. Tavito eats them with relish; Amadeo remembers the legless frogs struggling in the mud and refuses to eat. The father laughs. He leaves the house and disappears into the rain. His mother stops a moment and says, One less pest I have to worry about.

Julia has disappeared from Amadeo's room and the print of the mountains draws his attention. He has not seen mountains like that anywhere, jagged masses of rocks smeared with snow. They rise out of a flat landscape where the trees are in the process of changing color. Fall up north, he thinks, the way he remembers the Catskills. In Florida leaves stay on trees all year round. The weather is warm through October then turns downward a bit. In December and January the northers come, cold and rainy, and in February the winds of Lent. By March it is hot again. Once he saw it snow in Tampa. Tropical snow. The dogs were howling all through the neighborhood and the pigs ate sand. Rubén came home with a welt on his face where a snowball hit him. While the snow lasted, Amadeo thought that all the dirt and grime of the world had been erased. He and Julia danced in the snow and they packed buckets and turned them upside down to make a snowman, but Pastor jumped off the porch onto the mound and flattened it. Overnight the whiteness melted and they went on with their lives as if nothing had ever interrupted it. Is that the way life is, he asks, a long flat line with occasional moments of excitement that interrupt and throw you off the line, and all you can do is crawl yourself back to it and hope it is still there, straight and predictable? Here in Santa Gertrudis he looks forward to the interruptions, today especially that Nurse has gone to the beach and Nurse II and Orderly are flirting with each other and don't bother to check on him. By the time the sun sets Amadeo is hungry. It must be suppertime and they have forgotten to feed him. This is the kind of place his sons chose for him. The nurses don't care if the patients eat or not, live or not. If he could get up, if he could only use his voice, he would tell them exactly how he feels. He'd demand to be taken away. They lounge around and make eyes at each other while the patients starve. Where are his sons? Where is his family? As Amadeo's anger increases so does a feeling inside him that the world is moving away from him at blinding speed. His sons have forsaken him, his friends are dead. People go on with their lives: They renovate their living rooms, they cook, they go to the beach, they play their guitars, but he is reduced to a series of physical functions that he can no longer control. The story is almost over and as the world retreats, memory rushes in to replace it and along with it a self-pity he cannot control. It oozes out of him, it makes him drool, it blears his sight so that the snowy mountains become an underwater landscape.

How many hours does he wait for food? Time has a way of contracting and elongating so that minutes become hours and hours become whole afternoons. Time is relative, he remembers that from Einstein, but he doesn't believe it. He believes what his stomach tells him: time to eat. He tries not to think of mango; he thinks of liver and prune, he thinks of mud from the bottom of the Almendares River. As the day darkens and the shadows begin to invade the room he becomes convinced that Nurse II and Orderly are sick of him and are trying to starve him to death. It is late, very late. He needs to be changed, he needs to be moved, but no one comes. The place is death. Amadeo is alone in all the whiteness, with dark seeping in. It must be they are tearing down Santa Gertrudis. They have moved all the patients to a new facility and left him behind. He waits for the wrecking ball to come crashing down on him. Amadeo is blinking furiously and saliva is sloshing out of his mouth. There is a noise like a huge machine grinding bones, there are jackhammers, truck engines rumbling, his chest about to burst, then the jingling of the food cart outside the door. Nurse II comes in with the tray, places it on the rolling table, and attaches the bib around his neck. She is short with long black hair that she ties back in a ponytail. Her face is deeply scarred from acne. When she reaches for one of the jars on the tray, Amadeo notices that her fingers are stubby and that she is missing half of her left thumb. Were he not so hungry this would spark his curiosity. Where have you been, Nurse II? You tormenting me? Not much of a talker, this one (locuaz, he thinks, no es muy locuaz que digamos). Amadeo can count on the fingers of one hand the things she has said to him. The first time she spoke to him she called him a helpless soul. The second time she wished him a Merry Christmas before inserting a suppository into him. The third time, not really speaking to him but to herself, she wished him a speedy death and called him viejo putrefacto, rotten old man. She prods his lips with the spoon and he opens his mouth, then shuts it quickly. He is immediately revolted by what he tastes and pushes it right out. Damn, he wants to say. Carajo! What are you feeding me? She scoops the paste that remains on his lower lip, refills the spoon and jabs his lips again. This time he keeps his mouth shut and she forces the spoon in. It tastes like a dead animal marinated in urine, like the lower intestines of a leper, like the scrapings of an abandoned outhouse. Amadeo tries to read the label on the jar but her stubby hand is covering it. Nurse II is saying nothing, not this time. She takes the little teddy bear filled with juice and pushes the tip into his mouth. He tastes apple, his favorite, and sucks until he has drunk about half. She picks up the jar with the black paste again. He tries to warn her by blinking but she persists one last time, jamming the spoon into his mouth as deeply as it will go. He gags and spits it out. As she wipes his face with a corner of the towel he notices the watch on her wrist reads 11:02. He closes his eyes, distraught by the taste that has entered his mouth, spread up his olfactory canal, and blossomed in his brain. Bereft and hungry, suffocating with helplessness, he has nowhere to turn but to the picture of the mountains before him in which he envisions Nurse II walking, silent, stupid, indifferent until the only thing visible is the speck of her ponytail halfway up a snowy crag. Fall, he thinks, and she does.

Soon after Nurse II leaves the room, Orderly comes to change him. There is a nervous way about him whenever he enters, as if he were doing something illegal. Amadeo thinks he should start drooling just to unsettle him more but decides against it. Instead he follows Orderly's actions as he pulls off the covers, turns him over, wipes him, and puts on a clean diaper. No drooling today, Orderly asks. You learned your lesson, you did. And don't you mess with me again or I'm going to whip you. Whip all you want, negro de mierda, I won't feel it. Amadeo keeps from drooling and instead blinks forcefully several times. Orderly looks at him through cold, unfeeling eyes, unbuckles his belt and slaps it across Amadeo's belly, then brings it down the other way and slaps him again. Amadeo blinks faster now, daring Orderly to do it again. Orderly calls him a sick piece of dead flesh, fat old motherfucking scumbag cocksucking turd and just as he runs out of epithets, Amadeo starts slobbering, tightening his lips and slurping the saliva out so that a creamy froth dribbles down

his lower lip and chin. Eyes wide open, Orderly is screaming son of a sow, disgusting dog-shit-eating asshole faggot
dried-out-crusted-over slop bucket. Amadeo hasn't felt this
good in years, blinking and slobbering with all his will to
drive Orderly mad, and he succeeds better than he thought.
Orderly is doing a dance of rage around the room, screaming at the top of his lungs when he jumps on top of Amadeo
and wraps the belt around his neck. Nurse II reenters the
room and seeing Amadeo's face turning red and his eyes
bulging out of their sockets, grabs Orderly by the shoulders and hurls him off the bed. Amadeo has never seen such
a thing. Orderly is struggling to get up and calling him a
monster, a white devil, a fat-ass zombie; he is crawling out
the door while Nurse II, who has a fierce look on her face
like a vicious Latin terrier, pummels him around the head
and ears. Some time later several people come to visit
Amadeo: a man in a blue suit he has seen only once before, the bald doctor who is checking his blood pressure,
the physical therapist, and a blond woman holding a clipboard. He is fine, the doctor says, no harm done. The man
in the dark suit looks at his watch. There is no need to call
the police, then. Miss Argyle, he says to the blond, I want
that man fired immediately. Physical Therapist is going on
about Orderly, claiming he knew all along there was something wrong with him; the doctor is saying that Amadeo

will survive all of them the way he is going, he has the heart of an eighteen-year-old, and the blond woman, after writing something in her clipboard, asks the man in the dark suit if the family should be notified. He answers absolutely not and leaves. The other three stand around uncomfortably a moment before following him out. Amadeo is surprised by the feeling of relief he experiences when he is left alone. A long time passes—it seems a week—before Nurse II reappears bearing a tray of food. The paste she feeds him this time tastes of tar but he is so hungry he swallows it quickly. She follows that with banana and as he takes the last spoonful he notices her watch says 5:30. If he can survive a week, he can survive a month, if he can survive a month, he can do so forever. Imagine that: Amadeo the Immortal. He blinks gratefully at Nurse II, who changes him and pulls down the blinds for the night.

In the dark his tongue strains at language, language from inside his chest, gruff or gentle words, severe or soft, syrupy or dry as talcum powder, like fish, like rabbits, like an army of spiders scattering over the landscape. He tries to say tomorrow but he thinks Gomorrah, tries to say preacher and thinks prick her. Mania appears as Mañara, the surname of a literary playboy. Desire—for women, for money, for work, for respect—has made Amadeo an exile from himself. He knows he has lost the narrative of his life and all he has left is the flotsam of memory and language, which move inside him like figments of the past. He remembers how small stick figures repeated themselves on white paper, one with chestnut hair and black mouth, another green with yellow eyes, one with four arms, another with a smile from eye to eye, the last one bearing something blue like happiness on her shoulders. She was the most distant. He tried many tricks to get close to her—wearing a hat in the morning, going barefoot in the afternoon, playing games, working hard, being faithful to his wife, not being faithful. He drank good wine and rode around in fancy cars. He had his head shaved like a penitent and then let his hair grow like a bohemian. She remained distant, encouraging him to continue with his snares that trapped only him, kept him from living his life—he was no father, he was no husband. He was a singón, a fucker, but not a lover. That is why she, the distant one, stayed away. Amadeo has lost all hope but for whatever comes to him during the day and flees from him at night. And language? It fills his head, it makes him slobber, it churns around in his stomach, but it refuses to come out of him. It lives on in his memory, tied to a scene or a consequence of something he did or neglected to do. From the darkness of his room, Amadeo Terra tries once again to think of the future, to see himself on the other side of the river that divides life from death, but all he can visualize is the same parched earth, the same circular roads, the cloud of dust that floats over him. How does it feel to be whipped, to be touched? He cannot remember.

Amadeo Terra, cigar roller, entered a cigar factory at twelve years of age. He was already the man who was to follow the boy. Somebody gave him a broom and he started sweeping. Later, when he had swept the floor of the factory twice, a roller called to him. He was a thick-lipped mulatto with a round face and red kinky hair. How much did the boss say he was paying you? He didn't say. You working for free? The mulatto took five cents out of his pocket and gave it to him, then went over to the foreman. Now you will be paid, the mulatto said when he sat back down. And don't be a verraco. Nobody works for free. This is how he started, sweeping floors, watching the rollers at their job and listening to Elpidio. Amadeo learned to tell the good leaf from bad, which leaf burned right, which left. If you wanted to make a good cigar you couldn't cheat on filler and wrapper. Sooner or later you would hear from the other rollers, who would no sooner roll a bad cigar than cheat on their mothers. Not that they were saintly men by any means, but in the world of tobacco a man is judged by his ability at the rolling bench and by his capacity for work. If a man is a cheat that doesn't matter; if he is an adulterer, no matter, or an abuser or a thief or a street thug or an alcoholic. As long as he is a good roller, he is respected, and he is treated properly and with deference. In the solitude and darkness of his room Amadeo understands many things that passed him by when he had all his faculties. He understands, for example, that a man will pick a profession according to his station in life, and there was none better for him than being a cigar roller, un torcedor: a vocation of smoke in tune with his life, with anybody's life.

Elpidio the mulatto sat him at a table in his house and taught him the art of rolling a cigar. In time Amadeo learned how to identify the precise moment when the product began to take shape in his hands. Elpidio called it la vitola, the spirit of incipient perfection, which drove you to roll not one cigar but a dozen, a hundred, all the same shape, the same size. Defy God and do it every day for a lifetime. Elpidio did not give him talent—that he brought with him—but technique and work, work until he was so tired he couldn't see at night and the hands took over with their own will, and he worked some more and dreamed he was asleep and sleeping he worked until he woke and found himself working still. Elpidio and his wife Lala let him sleep in the larder among sacks of onion and rice with slabs of tasajo and bacalao suspended over him, on a canvas cot that smelled of the Spanish soldier Elpidio bought it from. He heard noises at night, creatures scurrying around on the floor. Rats, he didn't mind rats. It was spiders he dreaded and spent a sleepless first week making sure there were none in the larder. Lala fed him huge plates of roast pork, rice and beans, and boiled plantains, seven days a week without any variation because Elpidio ate nothing else. You can't roll cigars on an empty stomach, Elpidio liked to say while he sat at the table consuming plate after plate of food his wife dutifully placed before him. A man needs meat on his bones, he added. What good is the meat on his bones now, Amadeo asks himself. All Elpidio ever wanted was to stuff himself with all the food Lala could prepare. A strange ambition, Amadeo thinks, that he himself adopted. The difference was that he hungered for much more than food. In the two years he lived with Elpidio and Lala he gained seventy pounds and grew eight inches so that he towered over his teacher. He also became a better cigar roller than Elpidio, which is the primary reason he left the house, since you cannot stay with a teacher once your talent has surpassed his. When Amadeo walked out the front door for the last time, he could feel Lala behind him trying to hold back her tears.

He hears a soft but persistent noise at the window, a rasp, a peck, he can't exactly tell. If there were wind he would blame it on the wind; if there were a tree outside he would blame it on a branch tapping the glass, or a little bird that has landed on the window ledge, or an angel who wants to be let inside. He takes a deep breath and holds it to see if he can hear the noise better, but the noise won't come again. Instead he hears the beating of his heart increasing in intensity until he cannot hold his breath any longer and lets it go. As he does so, he feels his chest deflate, and he is suddenly afraid that if he doesn't breathe in immediately his soul will disappear. He inhales deeply and his soul settles back wherever the soul resides.

When Amadeo came home from Elpidio's house, his father was waiting for him with the one-way passage to Campeche. There were no embraces, no greetings for the returning son. Now you will know what hardship is, Amadeo remembers him saying. Half a foot taller than his father, Amadeo looked down at his flushed face. There was sweat streaming down his temples and blue veins swelling the forehead, and for a moment Amadeo was afraid, but the fear left almost immediately and was replaced by a deep disdain. Little did the old man know the favor he was doing the son, who would have done anything, even join the insurrectionists, to get away from the old man. Amadeo did not acknowledge his father's words and walked past him to greet his mother.

He stayed in the house two days, surprised at how small everything seemed—his old bedroom where he could barely turn around without hitting the iron bed or the night table, the crowded living room, which not long ago had seemed cavernous, and the dining room, in which he had once run around freely chasing imaginary enemies, where he now had to walk sideways between the chairs and the wall in order to get to his seat at the table. In the morning of the third day he gave his brother Tavito twenty-five of the fifty pesos he had saved, packed a canvas bag with a few belongings and the food his mother had prepared, and left for the capital to sail to Yucatán.

Amadeo hears the noise at the window again. He tries to discern a pattern to the tapping—three quick taps followed by a slow one—then it changes to two fast followed by two slow and then to three solitary slow ones and a rasping noise like a stick rubbing against concrete. He remembers the time on Nurse II's watch: 5:30. a.m.? p.m.? How many days, weeks since that 5:30, how many minutes? What year is it, '44, '53? The tapping is gone and he hears rigging stretch in the wind, the prow cutting waves, the swish, the plash, the canvas flapping, sailors' voices and the squawk of the sea birds. Above them the fierce sun of the

Gulf. The two-masted schooner *Los Tres Hermanos* flies over the sea. Amadeo has never been on anything that fast before. He remembers the captain's name, Bernardino Torres. He is a friend of his father and has promised him to take good care of the son, and Amadeo is surprised to learn this from the captain, for he has never imagined his father could be the least concerned about his welfare or have friends of any sort. Square-shouldered and fierce, the captain has the weather-beaten look of the seafarer but he is dressed like a bookkeeper, with a tie and a dark vest on which hangs a gold chain. With easterly winds pushing them along, they make Telchac in twenty hours, Celestún at noon of the following day. The noise comes again and turns into an itch he can't scratch. He smells trees and the wind coming off the sea, hears hammering, tastes tar. He feels the brine cutting his face, the sun, lower now, burning his ears. In an hour, as the sun sets behind the land, they can see a thin line of shadowy houses along the shore with the lighthouse off the port bow. Amadeo reaches for the gunwale as he looks at the port, sad, almost deserted, bearing no comparison to the great port of Havana, the city that will grow inside him and which he will use to compare the cities he knows and find them lacking. The noise is a banging now, like that of a pylon driver, churning and lifting then giving off a great sigh as it falls again.

Underneath it there is a silence he tries to reach, as if his hearing were a mechanical sand shovel digging into the sea bottom. He is moving up and down with the boat, which has slowed almost to a stop, the shore a hundred yards away. He is holding on for dear life, the mate is yelling out orders, the captain astern looking up at the mast. Amadeo can make out the shape of the dock in the darkness, a black rectangular form that extends over the water. The voices of the men fall away and the ship docks. Amadeo is peering at a precipice of desolation he has never known before.

Morning and the benevolent shadow of Sor Diminuta come to him suddenly. Her smell wakes him and he hears the mellifluous language of her prayer. She knows what the others don't: that he thinks, that he sees, that he smells, that he hears. Buenos días, Sr. Terra, she says. ¿Qué tal pasó la noche? It is her voice, not his. ¿Está listo para el baño? A stiff, accented, measured Spanish, too proper, but Spanish nevertheless. It is an unexpected question, coming from someone who is hardly a lover of bathing. What he wants is to be held, soothed, told the sounds he hears in the night are echoes of his fear, of his happiness, of youth haunting his old age. Sor Diminuta begins disrobing him when the loud persistent hammering comes again. If she has noticed the noise she gives no sign. She has taken the sponge to him, scrubbing his body with unusual speed and dispatch. Why in such a hurry, Diminuta? Do you have a tryst with God? She does his neck, his shoulders and chest, then moves to his belly, which jiggles as she scrubs. If he could tell her to slow down, let her hands move to their own rhythm so that he can imagine their warmth, their weight. By the time she is done her upper lip is glazed with sweat. He would tell her, too, that the noise at the window is too much, it has to stop. Slow down, Diminuta. Let your hands go where they will do the most good. There, that's it. The pecking again, followed by rasping, then a single clap. Mother of Mary, there is a song coiling into him like smoke. Mother of Mary, this woman smells like a haystack. How does he know how a haystack smells? He remembers, he knows. If the wrapper tears when the cigar is lit, it is too dry. A biting taste means the filler is old. Mother of Mary. An uneven burn, what they call canoeing, means a poorly rolled product, or one that has lain too long in the same position. Not enough draw means a tight roll. There is something out there beyond the window wanting to get in. Mother of Mary. Language like smoke. The sister brings the rolling table closer. On it are two jars, one brown like her habit, the other yellow, and his heart skips a beat. Bean, sweet and earthy, he swallows every spoonful she offers. Then the glorious yellow he has waited for. It enters his mouth, spreads all over his body; he is aglow with the taste of mango. A flood of yellow courses through his veins, reaches his heart and glows there like a fructose sun. There is no happiness like his and he feels the elephant on his chest, language pressing down. Happiness and pain at once so that he doesn't know which is which, the joy of tasting mango, his childhood returning with every spoonful, or the elephant making it hard to breathe.

No, that elephant is not language, it is not fear or his country in his dim imagining or the grief of a poorly lived life. He realizes this with a spoonful of mango in his mouth—taste of sun and truth commingled, taste of time. The sun surrounds the words, the puddle of flesh in the white expanse of the bed. The sun rises, takes the route of the sky and leaves. He knows it will return tomorrow, that it will serve again as the lantern of his days, but the final night is eternal. What's that? The final night is eternal. Stop the melodrama. Amadeo cannot tell if the voice he hears is Diminuta's or his own, or a combination of the two. Night is a physical phenomenon, not a metaphysical one. The rest is the anguish of a human being about to die. The world is in me. I moved like a top, doing what I had to do. You are not a top. They say every human is the world. Oriental foolishness. You are an infinitesimal point in the universe, or, if you prefer, you are that line that has always obsessed you. You began in A and now you are arriving at B, your final destination. Linear? Linear, circular, who cares. How about the emotions—fear, love, hate, envy, egoism, joy, avarice, lust? All can be reduced to two: love and fear. Love drives you to the fire, fear keeps you from putting your hand in it. Many times I have burned myself knowing I was going to burn myself. Some people burn themselves only a little. Others completely. Accept it or not, you are a member of the first group. In other words, you are neither mystic nor saint. To be a member of those clubs you have to throw yourself fully into the fire. Amadeo doesn't know what to say. What happened? I don't know. Yes, you do. A long time has passed. Or none. That door is shut. It must be opened. I was not well. That we know. I came home in a mood. Alfredo González, a union captain, asked for my resignation and denounced me before the membership. He said I was taking money from the owners. I went at him, but the others held me back. Alfredo, the consumptive who was nothing but skin and bones. If I had caught him, I would have snapped his body in two. Amadeo feels his throat tighten. Alfredo, whose wife drenched him in kerosene and set him on fire while he slept because he had been unfaithful to her. Diminuta, don't leave me. Amadeo's eyes cloud up and the noise outside the window has become like a scream or the aspiration of a huge mouth that is sucking him in. I am dying. You have been dying a long time. And you? Don't worry about me. I have God. What happened? He fell. Albertico. He did not fall. I arrived home in a rage, as if someone had injected fire in my veins. At this moment Amadeo feels the opposite, a frozen substance in his body and a scared hen fluttering about in his head. Albertico was running around the kitchen playing one of his games, making a nuisance of himself. His mother kept telling him to stop, that he was going to tip over a pot, but the boy wasn't listening. I took him by the arm and threw him against the wall like a rag doll. His head hit the corner of the windowsill. He fell motionless to the floor. He didn't actually fall; he slid like liquid down the wall. Something I couldn't control took possession of me. I threw the china closet to the ground. Julia was boiling water on the stove. I took the pot by the hot handles and threw it out the window. I wrecked the kitchen. The pots came down. I turned the stove over. I opened the cupboards and emptied their contents on the floor—flour, sugar, beans—and Albertico on the floor with his eyes unfocused, staring at nothing. On his nostrils there was a small bubble of blood growing. It popped and started, then it popped again and stopped altogether. Julia was kneeling next to him slapping his hand, trying to revive him. She realized her efforts were useless and gave me a look that contained all the disdain and hatred of the world. That is not all. The story about Julia becoming a curandera is a lie. Yes. A subterfuge. What is that? A way of avoiding the truth. Yes. You made it up to cover your shame and your guilt. All those people came to the house to pay their respects, not to solve their problems. Yes. Julia did not go crazy. She loved you. Yes. Underneath her hatred of you there was all that love—broken, battered, ground to useless dust. She couldn't afford to stay with you. Diminuta, you are all I have left. You have yourself. Amadeo can no longer swallow and he begins to slobber. His breathing becomes labored. The noise is an intolerable hum that is pouring out every cell of his body. I killed him. Your own son. My own flesh and blood I never loved. I have never loved anyone. Not even yourself? No. And Julia? And your other children? No. And they knew it. That's why they never visit. Can I rest? No. Death is not like that, it has nothing to do with rest. But this hospital, the nurses, the other patients. That is your reality and you have to live with it for the rest of your life, which could last one day or many. Then I am not dead yet. You're not, but look at yourself. You can't move, you can't talk, you can't control your bowels. You can't even swallow your spittle. But I produce it. I drool therefore I am. ¡Coño! Babeo ergo sum. Amadeo remains quiet a while, watching Diminuta put the cap back on the mango jar, the salve of his salvation. I am leaving now, Mr. Terra. Don't go, he says. No te vayas. I will not be coming back, but my prayers will be with you. I will not live without you, Diminuta. She has gathered the jars, the juice bottle, the bib, and the towels and looks at him one last time. Somewhere in her eyes there are tears for him but they are not coming forth. He calls that other voice, the one that made all this up, but it does not respond. His eyesight becomes blurred as if he were underwater. The noise in his body is driving him crazy. Amadeo is swimming in the great ocean of sadness and destitution. It is a gray sea with uniform waves that repeat themselves toward an indefinite horizon. Just beyond his reach are the faces of Chano, his parents, Julia, Albertico, all the dead he has known. He swims toward them to touch them, to say to them what he is feeling and what he kept himself from feeling. His sorrow is greater than anything he has ever experienced. The elephant is pressing down on him, but he continues swimming, no matter that he can barely breathe. His head goes under, then comes up again. He is swinging his arms wildly, kicking his legs. There is no solution. Just as he is getting close to the faces they dip under the surface and reappear a few yards away, nearer the horizon, the darkness, the silence. His lungs are filling with water. He can hear it bubbling inside as he tries to take in air. His eyesight clears a moment and he discovers that all those faces floating in the gray sea, all those eyes, all those mouths, are identical. It is his face he is looking at, himself he is reaching for.

Acknowledgments

For help in researching and understanding the cigar industry and the community of Ibor City, I am indebted to Dr. Ferdie Pacheco, "The Fight Doctor," the late Adela Gonzmart of the Columbia Restaurant, and the late Tony Pizzo, the official historian of Tampa. My special thanks also go to the staff of the Special Collections of the University of South Florida, where I spent many fascinating hours looking over unpublished materials dating back to the early history of Tampa.

I have been employed by New School University and the MFA Program for Writers at Warren Wilson College for several years now. Institutions are made of people and the people at both these institutions—students, faculty, and staff—continually grace me with their support and help make the practice of writing a little less solitary, a little less daunting.

Among the people who read this manuscript and offered valuable suggestions are my father, Pablo, who reads everything I write and tells me, honestly, or as we say in Cuban, sin pelos en la lengua, whether he likes it or not, that other Pablo, my son, and my sister Silvia. My former editor Karen Braziller and my agent Elaine Markson, too, encouraged me in the usual ways and in ways I am just now beginning to understand. There are few people in the book business who love good literature as much as they do.

I am especially fortunate to be working with Elisabeth Schmitz, my editor at Grove/Atlantic. People know of her talents as an editor, but not everyone is aware of the generosity, intelligence, and care that inform her editorial suggestions. Elisabeth knows, and she knows that she knows. That makes her a wisewoman in the realm of fiction.

Finally, I must thank my wife, Beth. She did all of the above. She also had to tolerate the moods, the quirks, the frustrations, the panic and manic attacks, and all the other byproducts that come with writing a novel. She is next to me always and that makes all the difference.